# The Shorty Collection

## Love Stories in Various Lengths

Lacey Ray

ISBN: 9798839675384

# DEDICATION

Cutie Pie, I should just call this the cutie pie collection because I wrote the majority of these stories just for you, but I won't. I still get a little nervous when I share my work with you because I value your opinion but you always have something positive to say even when the story is rough and needs polishing. I appreciate your encouragement and excitement over my writing and I know I have improved as a writer since meeting you. You might not know it but you've taught me a lot. Love you lots, Cutie Pie!

# CONTENTS

# ACKNOWLEDGMENTS

JustCMe, my beautiful angel baby, thank you for writing the song used in *He Is Mine* and for being an inspiration for the character of Cee. You took my pathetic attempt at songwriting and made it wonderful!

Brittaney Joy, you have did it again! Looked inside my brain and gave me a beautiful cover. Thank you so much for working with me.

Alice, I adore you! Thank you for your support and friendship. You help me take my words and turn them into something I'm very proud of.

# HE IS MINE

## BARAMEE

"You want me to do what?"

I must have heard him wrong. He can't just hit me with shit like this twenty minutes after stepping off the stage of the final concert in the last leg of my world tour. All I want to do is take a shower, eat some food, and find a soft mattress to crash on for ten days straight. Not necessarily in that order. My brain cannot process crazy talk right now.

"The XYZ Network wants you for a new project they have coming up. It starts in a month."

"Billy! I have been on the road for six months. You promised me that I would have at least three weeks of downtime before I had to get out of bed," I whine. "I've been working nonstop since I was fifteen. I'm tired."

"Boo hoo. Baramee, you're only twenty. You can rest when you're dead."

My manager is a cruel, cruel man.

"What is this project exactly?"

"A gay soap opera."

I sit up and look at him dumbfounded. "Excuse me? You want me to act in a soap opera? Like one of those day time drama filled train wrecks that my gram and ma would watch every day like clockwork. I don't know how many times I had to hear about that hussy Erica Kane marrying a new man, but that didn't stop gram from watching."

"Sort of. The network is trying something new. It will be a nightly soap that revolves around the lives of three friends who happen to be gay," Billy explains.

"Don't I have to audition? I've never acted before."

"The part of Nex was written just for you."

"Really?! What if I refuse?" I'm feeling bratty. I have really been looking forward to being a couch potato for three months.

Billy gives me a look and I roll my eyes. Yeah, like I'm going to refuse.

***

"We will be there in an hour. Try to get some sleep."

I glance at Billy and nod. I am beyond exhausted. When Billy said the project started next month, he really meant the month two days from then. If I didn't love the man like a brother I may have killed him and buried his body somewhere. Not only do I not get to be a lazy ass couch potato for three weeks I don't even get to do it for three fucking days! The last three days have been a whirlwind of visiting my parents and sister for too short a time and getting myself together to move to Chicago to work on a project that is out of my element. Don't get me wrong. I'm excited, but this could very well be a total disaster.

I trust Billy. Billy has never steered me wrong from the moment we met when I was hitting my pre-teens. Such a fun age. I am one of those You Tube successes. Don't judge me! I didn't start the channel to try and get famous. I'm actually painfully shy if you can believe it. My mom suggested that I try and get out of my shell by singing. So I joined the choir in school and sang at church. For those several minutes I stand onstage it's like a switch is flipped and I become a different person. I don't have stage fright, the notes come out clear, and I feel alive. Once I step off the stage I go back to being me. A turtle, pulling my head into my shell whenever anyone talks to me. Billy discovered me when I was thirteen, but my mom wanted me to wait until I was a little older to jump into anything that had the potential to make me grow up way too fast. Three months before I turned sixteen I signed a record deal and the rest as they say is history. I haven't stopped since. I don't regret anything.

As we make our way to the studio to do a meet and greet I re-look over the first script. The tentative name of the soap is 'Too Fab For Words'. To me it sounds like a makeover show. I really hope they change it.

The summary read like this:

*'Too Fab For Words' revolves around the lives of three best friends from high school James, Nex, and Gage. When pop star Nex gets outed and dumped all on the same day he is whisked home so his management can do damage control and he can nurse his broken heart. James and Gage rush home to help their friend and to them helping is raising a little hell and finding him someone to fall in love with.*

Do you want the sad truth? I am a twenty year old virgin that has never been kissed. How did I reach the age of twenty being a pop singer without ever being kissed you ask? I knew pretty young that I was gay and I had no interest kissing random guys for the sake of just kissing them. I wanted my first kiss to be special and being in the business that I'm in I have to be careful about who I let into my life. There also happens to be the fact that I'm not out. My family and closest friends know and I'm not going to lie if ever asked directly but surprisingly in this day and age of nosy questions, reporters and talk show hosts have not out and out asked. I can feel that it is coming and I'm fine with it, but not having to answer a bunch of personal questions the past few years has been nice. I got around the girlfriend question by shyly answering that I was focusing on school and my career. Which had been the truth.

After meeting HIM I am kicking myself for never having dated. I have no game.

***

"I would like to welcome everyone to 'Too Fab For Words' meet and greet. We will be getting started in just a moment."

"I hope they change the name," the voice beside me whispers with a wink.

"It does sound like we are going to be giving straight guys make overs," I agree with a laugh.

His eyes widen in delight and a dimple pops when he smiles. I recognize him as the actor playing James.

"I love your music! I've been to several of your concerts. I hope I don't sound like a crazy fanboy. Name's Keene by the way." Wow, Keene is hyper.

"I like your movies so I guess we are even."

"Keene! Dude! I was so excited when my manager said that you agreed to work on this."

When I turn to find the voice my breath gets caught in my throat. When I was given the cast information and the script not everyone had been secured yet. One character that had been TBD was Gage. Looking at him I know he is Gage and he happens to be one of the male actors that I find hot as hell. How the fuck am I going to be able to concentrate with him around?

“Baramee...Baramee...Dude!”

Geez I’m already spacing out.

“Sorry...it’s Bam.”

“....”

Looking at their confused expressions I need to explain. “You can call me Bam. My little sister couldn’t pronounce Baramee. Her favorite show at the time was the Flintstones and she would always look at me and go ‘Bam-Bam’. Bam stuck and everyone started calling me it.”

“That’s really cute. I’m Kite. Since the three of us are about to become on screen besties, let's be friends.”

Taking the offered hand I shake it, biting back a moan at the feel of his skin on mine. He’s even more gorgeous in person. I want to reach out my hand and brush the hair out of his eyes and run the tip of my finger down his cheek to see if his skin is as soft as I think it is. I’m in so much fucking trouble.

Friends? Sure, we could start with that.

***

"You're staring at him again."

I look up to see Kind standing over me with an all knowing smile on her face. Kind plays Abby, my older sister, on the show and she is pretty kick ass. We are in a boot camp of sorts for two weeks getting to know each other and for me who has never acted before getting the chance to learn some acting techniques. While I had been nervous the first day I quickly was put at ease. The guys I will be working with the most are all very cool and I'm grateful. It would have sucked royally to have to work with a bunch of shitheads.

"Am I that obvious?"

"A little but I've seen that lovesick expression many times. When you start to have your romantic scenes with Fen just think of HIM and the audience is going to go crazy," Kind recommends.

My eyes automatically seek Kite out. He is in the middle of doing an exercise with Boss who plays his love interest Zee. I won't lie. I'm a little jealous. What I wouldn't give to be Boss at that very moment wrapped up in Kite's arms. Is it too late to switch roles with Boss? Damn...

Unlike daily soap operas that run pretty much all year round our show is going to have seasons. The network has ordered one season of twenty episodes, which is four weeks of airtime since forty five minute episodes will be airing daily Monday through Friday. The network is also trying something different by completely shooting all the episodes before the first episode premieres. I'm used to long days but I think they are trying to kill us by filming one episode every five days. This is a seriously tight schedule. I really don't understand why they seem to film the episode out of order. Why start with the dramatic ending that I'm not even worked up to yet, just to finish with the lukewarm beginning? If I wasn't so virginal I'm sure I would think that is some kind of fucked up foreplay.

"Bam! I know it's been a long day but try to focus."

I'm focusing. Just not on what I'm supposed to be focusing on. This is week two of filming and we are in the middle of episode 13. I'm telling you it is crazy how they do this. In this particular scene me, James, and Gage are at a club and they have pushed me into the arms of the guy they believe will cure me of my heartache. Fen, who plays Ollie, my love interest on the show, is a total sweetheart. We are about the same height, he has short dark hair that gets styled out of his stunning chocolate brown eyes, and his smile can light up a room. Even as we are dancing together to the slow music playing in the background my eyes keep wandering to HIM. Did wardrobe really have to dress him in those tight, holey jeans that hug his ass perfectly? The dark blue t-shirt that is clinging to his taut muscles is making my palms itchy to run them under the soft fabric and caress his skin. Shit...I think I may be drooling.

"Bam! Stop looking over at Keene and Kite. In this scene Nex is finally letting go and giving Ollie a chance. You dance and share your first kiss."

Kiss! I hadn't read anything in the script about kissing in this scene. I thought that came in episode 15, which I know we aren't shooting for another couple weeks. I need time to prepare myself. I'm not thrilled to be having my first kiss on screen with a guy I barely know, but I'm prepared to be professional about it.

"Didn't you read the re-write?"

"No," I whisper. Billy told me that there had been a slight change but not to worry about it since the lines stayed the same. He really didn't value breathing. I would kill him slowly, over days.

"Are you feeling okay, Bam? Your face is flushed," Fen asks, placing his palm against my forehead. "You're burning up."

"You all have worked really hard tonight. Let's stop here and we will resume on Monday. Bam get yourself checked out. I know you have a concert tomorrow."

I nod my head and Billy is there to whisk me away. I'm sick all right. Lovesick. That has me acting a fool. Now I'm embarrassed over the fact I have been called out blatantly staring at my crush. Kite is quickly becoming my obsession. We are total opposites. While I'm shy and quiet, he is loud and flirty. At least with him being friendly as hell I didn't have to worry about talking. He could talk your ear off and I could listen to him all day long. See, fucking lovesick.

"Do I need to call your doctor? You have to do that concert tomorrow Bam."

"I'm not sick you traitor. You could have warned me," I seethe shooting daggers at Billy.

"I didn't want to tell you about the kiss and freak you out. It's inevitable," Billy shrugs unrepentant.

"Then I guess I need to find a fan tomorrow to practice my kissing on."

Billy raises his brow, "Don't get cheeky."

"Don't omit things again."

"Deal."

***

The heat from the stage lights is making me sweat. I can feel the sweat sliding down my back, but I don't care about how wet my t-shirt is getting. On stage in front of a sold out crowd no matter the size is a heady feeling. The beat of the music vibrates through my body as I dance my way around the stage. I can never stay still when I sing fast songs. I barely can stay still when I sing slow songs. I usually have to sit down.

"I want to thank everyone for coming out tonight! I know the weather ended up being yucky, but I'm so glad to spend the evening with you. To make it worth your while having had to negotiate rain slick roads I have a surprise for you."

The arena becomes a roar as my guest steps out on the stage.

"I think they might recognize you Hannah," I say with a laugh.

"Looks like. What's up beautiful people?! Hasn't my buddy Bam been fantastic so far?"

Once again the crowd goes wild. I would never get tired of that I didn't think.

"I have been fortunate enough to record a couple of songs with the lovely Hannah over the past couple of years and as long as it's okay with all of you we would like to sing them for you now…"

Yeah, I didn't think they were going to say no.

"Thank you so much! You have been great. See you again soon!"

I jog off the stage and am grateful it is over. I'm dead tired.

"That was a lot of fun Bam. It has been great seeing you," Hannah says, giving me a hug.

"You too Han. Maybe next time we can actually have time to catch up. Be safe on your flight home. Call me."

“I will.  I can’t wait to see you on TV.”

After grabbing a quick shower I settle myself on the couch and call my sister.  I have a little time to kill before Billy will drive us back to the apartment we are staying in.

“Bam!  How did the concert go?  Have you stopped being a bitch and talked to HIM yet?  Come on Bam man up and grow some balls.”

I can see myself in the mirror and my smile is wide. It is hard not to smile when I talk to my baby sister. She isn’t a baby anymore at eighteen, but she will always be my little sister.  We are close, best friends.  I can talk to her about anything.

“The concert was great.  No.  Did you just call me a bitch AND tell me to grow a pair all in the same breath?  Harsh, sis.”

“You said he’s flirty.  He can’t be hard to talk to.”

“He’s flirty with everyone,” I say frowning in annoyance.  He didn’t have to be so fucking friendly with everyone.

“What’s the worst thing that can happen?”

“Humiliating rejection.”

My sister sigh’s.  “Bam, that just comes with the territory of putting your heart out there.  How many times have you listened to me cry over boys?  Each boy is part of my love story and I don't regret those tears."

"Well I'm now regretting that my love story is blank because I'm going to experience my first kiss on screen. Your older brother is pretty pathetic huh," I groan throwing my head back on the back of the couch.

"No, Bam. You are pretty special. I miss you."

"Miss you too, Bug. Think I can find someone to kiss before Monday?"

***"Me…"***

I know that voice. It has started to invade my dreams. Holy Shit it is HIM...

## KITE

"Has my career come to this where you have signed me up for an evening soap opera that will probably get canceled before the fifth episode airs?" I grumble to my manager.

"Gage was written with you in mind.  It's perfect for you," Malik says.

"Perfect doesn't always mean good."

"Kite, just give it a chance.  Keene is signed on and that pop singer Baramee."

My heart skips a beat at hearing that name. Baramee came on the scene at the tender age of sixteen.  I remember seeing him for the first time on one of those music shows and I had to sit down.  I was blown away not only by his voice, but by his beauty.  I was impressed with the way he spoke and carried himself.  It was so fucking cute at how shy he seemed.  As he was starting out at sixteen I was twenty-two and had been in this business since I was three.  I have been able to do what some child stars have not been able to, transition from working as a child to working as an adult.  He is twenty now but I haven't stopped aging.  I just turned twenty-seven.  Seven years seems like a huge age gap.

I need a hit. The last couple of projects I have been on weren't complete flops, but they weren't successes either. I'm getting to the point of wondering if this is worth it anymore. Knowing I would be working with HIM makes me want to give it one more shot.

***

The day of the meet and greet I'm nervous. Nervousness is a new feeling for me. When I see HIM sitting with Keene I feel a pang of jealousy. That is also a new feeling for me. Keene needed to get his ass out of my seat!

"Keene! Dude! I was so excited when my manager said that you agreed to work on this." That excitement is fading seeing him next to my cutie. Get a grip Kite. He isn't your anything.

When he turns to look at me I almost freeze. Pictures didn't do him justice. This kid is stunning. I am completely fucked.

"Baramee...Baramee...Dude!"

At least I'm not the only one zoned out. I bite my lip to keep from grinning because I'm pretty sure he is staring at me. That is equally exciting and equally frightening. I only half hear his story about why people call him Bam because I'm lost in how fucking cute he is.

"That's really cute. I'm Kite. Since the three of us are about to become on screen besties, let's be friends."

I hope we become so much more.

***

I find out quickly that Bam is extremely shy. How has he survived working in this business with his shy demeanor? I'm surprised he hasn't been chewed up and spit out. Watching him interact with our crew is my favorite thing to do. When he catches me looking he blushes the prettiest light pink color. I dream about how far that blush runs down his body. You can imagine the problem I wake up with every morning. I feel like a pervert dreaming about the barely legal cutie, but my brain, heart, and dick can't get on the same page.

"When you aren't teasing the poor kid you're staring at him. You like him," Kind teases as she sits across from me. We're in the middle of doing one on one exercises with the one who plays our love interest. Boss and I just finished ours and it is Bam and Fen's turn.

"I'm not hiding it very well am I?"

"I've known you since we were ten, Kite. I know you. Most would think you are just looking at him intently, but I know better."

Kind and I have worked together before. We first played siblings, then lovers, and now my best friend's sister. I know, it's weird but I love Kind and I would work with her on any project.

"I'm too old for him. Look how sweet and fresh he is."

Kind arches her eyebrow. "Yeah there is an age difference but it's not like you are a wizened old man. I think your open confident personality and his shy sweetness will complement each other well. Just ask him out."

"Dating a co-star is never a good idea. You know that better than anyone."

She smiles a sad smile. "It can end badly. Shane and I were able to be professional and go on and do two more seasons of Once in a Lifetime."

"But it was hell," I say softly.

Kind doesn't answer, she just pats my hand and watches Bam with Fen.

I'm already in hell. What I wouldn't give to be in Fen's shoes at that very moment, or maybe not. Even though Bam is wrapped up in Fen's arms his eyes are on me.

***

"I've heard that Bam has never been kissed," Keene says conversationally as we pack up our stuff to leave for the evening. We are renting a place together during filming since neither of us live in Chicago.

I stop and look at him in disbelief. "He's twenty. How the hell has he reached twenty without even kissing someone?"

Keene shrugs. "I don't know. It's just what I heard. I think that's why he clammed up so bad tonight at the thought of kissing Fen."

"I had my first kiss onscreen. It was with Kind actually. My first real kiss was with Saxton Roberts," I grin at Keene.

"Mr. I'm a supermodel Saxton was your first real kiss," Keene exclaims in surprise.

"He wasn't a supermodel then. Between you and me he's an awful kisser."

Keene cracks up hearing that. "He kept trying to find a mirror to look at himself in, didn't he?!"

"Something like that. I've kissed several more on and off screen since."

"You wouldn't mind popping that particular cherry for Bam…" Keene waggles his eyebrows comically at me, making me laugh.

"Maybe." I'm not admitting just how fucking badly I want it.

***

Watching Bam dance around the stage doing what he loves just might kill me. I want to run my hands all over him, sweat be damned. He is like a different person up there entertaining this massive crowd. Night and day. I love both sides of him.

"Stop tip toeing around him," Kind yells in my ear.

I'm only tip toeing because I don't want to hurt him. He's special. I can feel that he is different from any other guy I had dated and that terrifies me. I want to be all his firsts if it was true that he had never dated before. I want to take him on his first date. Be his first kiss. Be his first I love you.

Shit…

"There it is."

"What?" I shout.

"That smile you are sporting says it all. You have made your decision. As one of your close friends and Bam's 'sister' I give you my blessing. You aren't going to hurt him, Kite. At least not on purpose. Go get your man."

"My cutie," I say with a wink.

I give her a hug and she pushes me towards where I could go backstage. Bam has just finished the concert and I want to see him before his manager sweeps in and takes him away. I'm in luck when I find out that Billy has a few things to take care of and is giving Bam some time to relax. Once security sees my badge they clear me for entering his dressing room. I quietly close the door when I notice he is talking on the phone. I don't want to disturb him.

I can't hear who he is talking to but I can hear what he is saying. I think he is talking about me.

*"He's flirty with everyone."*

I can hear a lilt of annoyance in his voice. Jealous, cutie?

*"Humiliating rejection." Bam whines. I would be crazy to reject you*, cutie.

*"Well I'm now regretting that my love story is blank because I'm going to experience my first kiss on screen. Your older brother is pretty pathetic huh,"* he groans, throwing his head back on the back of the couch.

So that is true. You are far from pathetic my cutie. Dammit if that isn't a huge fucking turn on to be his first entry in his love story.

*"Miss you too, Bug. Think I can find someone to kiss before Monday?"*

***Like hell...***

"Me..." It is out of my mouth before I have time to think about it. No one is getting his first kiss but me.

When his head pops up off the couch his eyes are huge in recognition through the mirror. Along with the surprise I see excitement and hope in his eyes.

"I'm going to call you later, Bug. Love you," Bam says, eyes never leaving mine. He ends his call and stays frozen on the couch.

"Kiss me…" Wow I'm a regular Shakespeare right now.

Bam gets up slowly from the couch and walks over to stand in front of me.

"I'm probably going to suck at it," Bam says with a bite to his lower lip.

Not a fucking chance. But Seriously! How did this kid get to be such a fucking tease? SELF keep this on repeat. YOU CANNOT MOLEST THE TEMPTING BRAT. I am so completely fucked.

## BARAMEE

"I'm probably going to suck at it," I admit biting my lip. Why did I just admit that to HIM? Now he's going to know just how big of a loser I really am. Kite just smiles at me and hands over the single rose he has been holding.

"Not a chance, Bam." Kite takes a step closer to me and I stop breathing. If this is a dream I don't want to wake up.

The door slams open and Billy walks in carrying bags. "Let's go kid. I know you have to be tired."

Dead...he is so fucking dead.

Billy stops and looks between the two of us and gives me a knowing look. "Did I interrupt something?"

You know you did Mr. Smirky.

"No, I was just saying hi to Bam and telling him how much I enjoyed the concert. I wanted to see if he is free tomorrow," Kite says addressing Billy.

"Bam's available tomorrow."

"Great! See you around eleven tomorrow, Bam."

I shake my head yes. I'm too excited to talk.

Once Billy and I make it to our car I turn on him. "You are fired!"

Billy rolls his eyes and laughs. "You should be thanking me. My interruption got you a date."

I stick my tongue out at him. I'm not thanking him, but I did smile.

***

I'm in panic mode but it calms me down when my sister's face fills the screen of my computer.

"Geez, bro, it looks like your closet exploded in your room. What the hell is going on?"

"Kite is picking me up in an hour and I have nothing to wear!" I moan loudly.

"You finally grew some balls and asked him out!" my sister screams.

"He asked me," I mutter. "I think..."

"What?"

"Nothing. Help me out, Bug," I pleaded. My sister's name isn't Bug by the way. Her name is Beth, but our mom had always called her mama's little lady bug. I just copied her but dropped the little lady part. We became known as Bug and Bam.

"Where is he taking you?"

"Don't know." I really didn't care as long as it ended with him placing his delicious looking lips on mine.

"You can't go wrong with a pair of jeans, a t-shirt with a button down over it, and wear that leather bracelet I bought for you for your birthday. You'll have his tongue hanging out I guarantee it," Bug says with a wink.

After changing into my favorite pair of jeans with a few strategic holes and a light/dark green shirt combo I did a silly runway walk for my sister. She whistles and declares me good to go.

"Knock him dead Bam. Call me later. I want to hear all about it."

"You will be my first call, Bug. Thanks."

"Bam! Kite's here."

"Gotta go. Love you."

"Love you, too. Good luck." My sister blows me a kiss and disconnects.

As I step into the living room and see HIM sitting on the couch waiting for me I almost melt into a puddle of goo. How did that fucker make a pair of shorts and a tank top look so damn sexy? Is he trying to kill me? As his eyes meet mine and his lips twitch into a smirk I can see he knows exactly what he is doing.

"Ready to go?"

I nod my head yes and that just makes his smirk grow bigger. He is such a jerk for enjoying making me lose my words all the time.

Kite holds out his hand and I shyly place mine in his. Lacing our fingers together he pulls me close so he can talk straight into my ear, causing a shiver to run down my body.

"You look amazing, Bam. Yes, I like making you nervous."

I push him away blushing and mutter, "Jerk."

"Your jerk…"

I'm floating on air all the way to the car.

"Are you kidnapping me?"

Kite glances over at me and grins.

"Why? Are you scared?"

"No." I'm not. Even after being on the road for over an hour I'm in heaven just being this close to HIM. I had been afraid that I wouldn't know what to talk about with him and we would have awkward silence, but Kite is easy to talk to. It helped that it was just the two of us. I'm surprised that we have a lot in common.

“We will be there in a minute.”

True to his word we pulled into a massive parking area a few minutes later.
“Where are we?” I ask looking around.

“Farmers Market. Here,” Kite presses a floppy hat and sunglasses in my hand. “So people won’t recognize you so easily.”

I chuckle and place the hat on my head and slide the glasses onto my face. “How do I look?”

“Fucking adorable.”

“Kite!” I exclaim, cheeks burning in embarrassment.

He just grins, unrepentant, and puts on a ball cap and sunglasses. “Let’s go.”

“How do you know about this place? I love Farmers Markets. My mom makes soap and sells them at our Farmer’s Market back home.”

As we start walking down the first row of vendors Kite takes my hand and we stop to look at some jewelry.

“I have a slight confession to make,” he says while his head is down examining a bracelet. “I may have asked around to see what you like.”

At my silence he looks up to see my stunned expression. “I wanted to make sure that our first date was special.”

I lean in and kiss him on the cheek. I'm overwhelmed with his thoughtfulness and his kindness. That combined with him calling this a date is making me bold.

Kite touches his cheek and his eyes light up in awe.

"Thank you. You just taking the time to find out what I like is very special."

"Come on. Let's go see what else they have."

I'm suddenly very grateful that my love story has been blank and Kite is the first one being written in it.

**KITE**

I cannot remember a first date or any date for that matter being as fun as going to the Farmer's Market has been with Bam. If I'm being honest it isn't the Farmer's Market that I am enjoying, it's Bam. I love watching him explore each booth and see the way his eyes light up in joy or excitement. I love talking with him. Bam is funny. He has a great sense of humor.

"Can we get ice cream? I think I saw an ice cream parlor as we passed through town," Bam asks, giving me the cutest smile. Like I'm going to tell him no.

I should have told him no. This didn't look like an ice cream parlor, it looks like a sex toy shop. Who the hell names their ice cream parlor The Pink Whip? Is that an actual whip in their logo? As I am going to make the suggestion to go to another place Bam has already opened the door and is waiting for me to walk in with him.

"Hello! Welcome to the Pink Whip. Where we whip all our ice cream fresh every morning. Today's special is the pineapple whip, my personal favorite."

"My sweetheart does love his pineapple. My favorite is the chocolate caramel whip, but all of our whips are good."

Sweetheart, who apparently loved pineapple, is a handsome man with colorful tattoos on his arms. The other worker is also very handsome with smooth dark skin and a beautiful smile.

"You have so many," Bam says in amazement.

"Would you like to try some samples?"

Bam eagerly nods his head yes and I chuckle at his enthusiasm. When it comes to ice cream I know what I want. I like mint chocolate chip in a cone. Nice and simple. Soon Bam has four samples to try and he is doing obscene things with a tiny spoon.

"You look familiar. I can't quite put my finger on where I have seen you before," Daniel says, staring intently at my cutie.

"I have one of those faces," Bam says around a mouthful of ice cream.

It isn't that Bam has one of those faces, it's the fact that he has removed his floppy hat and glasses. It isn't going to take them long to recognize him.

"Cutie, have you decided?" I ask not to use Bam's name. Looking at me he smiles and nods.

"I'll have a vanilla whip dipped in sprinkles in a sugar cone."

After all those tasters he picks vanilla. He's so fucking cute.

As we head towards the door, treats in hand, the guy with the tattoos yells, "I got it! Babe! We just waited on Baramee. You know he's my hall pass."

"In your dreams he may be, but no way in hell am I ever sharing or giving you a pass sweetheart. You're mine."

"Oh babe…"

I look back to see "babe" kissing the hell out of "sweetheart". Okay...time to go.

"This is the best ice cream I've ever had," Bam moans.

I should not have looked. If I thought his spoon job had been obscene the way he is working that cone is downright pornographic. We need to sit down. I cannot walk around with a hard on. Walking over to a nearby bench we take a seat. Taking a bite of my ice cream I almost choke watching Bam eat his. With his tongue Bam steadily gives the cone little licks pushing the ice cream from the base of the cone to the tip. Once he makes one full turn of the cone the tip of the ice cream disappears between his full lips only for him to start the erotic process over. After the third full lick rotation and tip suck I can't take it anymore. I have to taste that teasing mouth. My cone forgotten I let it drop to the ground as I slide closer to the man that has invaded my heart. His sharp intake of surprised breath just spurns me on as I grip the back of his neck.

"Kite…"

My name on his lips sounds so sweet and I bet they are going to taste even sweeter.

As our lips touch for the first time I am overwhelmed by how right it feels. Don't laugh but it is like his lips were made for me. We fit together perfectly. I lick his lower lip teasingly seeking entrance and we both moan when our tongues meet. He tastes delicious. Partly like the vanilla ice cream and the other part is just all Bam.

"Is it always like this?" Bam pants.

"No." Cupping his cheeks I place light kisses on his forehead, cheeks, nose, and finally his lips. "I've never experienced a kiss like that. Only with you."

Bams smile makes my heart skip a beat. He is so fucking beautiful. He is so fucking mine.

"There are so many reasons why this isn't a good idea. We are co-stars. I'm older than you. You deserve so much better than me…"

"Stop! I know all the reasons and I don't care. The crappy reasons haven't stopped me from falling in love with you!" Bam's eyes grow big and his cheeks turn flaming red.

"You love me, cutie," I tease. He hits me and buries his face in my chest. I hear a muffled yes.

Wrapping my arms around him I whisper in his ear. "That's good because it would suck being in an unrequited love. Those blow."

"You really are a jerk you know that! You DON'T deserve me," Bam yells pushing at my chest his cute chubby cheeks scrunched up in anger.
I tweak his nose and kiss his angry pout. "It would have sucked for me, cutie. I'm sorry for making a bad joke. Baramee, you completely own me heart and soul. I love you."

Bam grins and bites his lip. "You're still a jerk."

"But I'm your jerk."

***

"Something is different about Bam today?" Keene observes as we wait for them to get everything in place to re-shoot the club scene.

I shrug and a smile plays on my lips. I know what's different but it isn't something I'm going to discuss with Keene. On the way home from our date yesterday we had a long talk about what happens next. I'm out, Bam isn't. While Bam is ready to come out I don't think it's the right time. It will be a lot for him to come out and also admit to being in a relationship with a co-star. My motives may be a little selfish. I just want him to myself for a little while.

"He seems more confident today," Boss agrees.

Bam and I spent part of the evening last night rehearsing his kissing scene with Fen. I would say that his confidence has been boosted. He just better not kiss Fen like he kissed me.

"Ok everyone places please. Scene 4, take 1, and in 3, 2, 1 ACTION!"

I watch as Bam dances with Fen. His eyes catch mine and I give him a wink.

"You guys are cute together," Keene whispers.

"Shut it."

"Seriously. I'm happy for you and my lips are sealed."

I take my eyes off Bam for a moment to look at Keene. I can tell he is genuinely happy for us and that he won't tell anyone.

"Thanks."

My eyes land back on Bam as Fen leans in for the kiss. It is just a brief brush of the lips but I hate it. I hate seeing someone else kiss my cutie.

"You better wipe that look off your face or everyone is going to know," Keene advises.

I can feel that my lips have twisted into a grimace so I smooth them out into a smile. Keeping us a secret maybe be harder than I anticipated.

**BARAMEE**

"Cutie!  You ready for our date?"

"Oh, Gage how long have you been standing there?" Zee asks embarrassed being caught lost in thought.

"Long enough to see you chew the tip of that eraser clean off. Really, Zee, what has that poor defenseless bit ever done to you? So vicious." Gage winks at Zee teasingly.

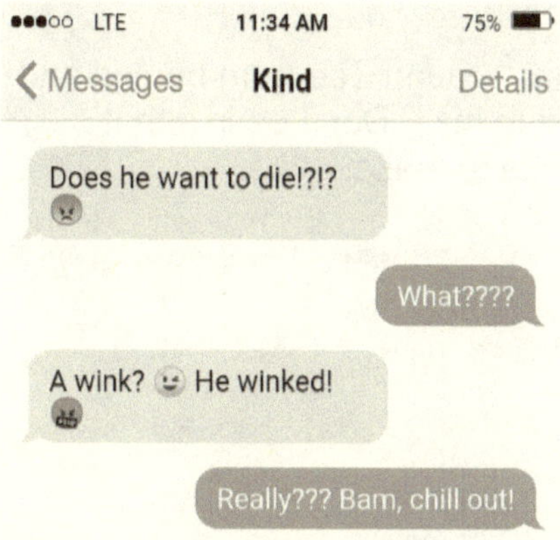

Zee hits Gage playfully and makes room for him on the bench he is sitting on. "Just lost in thought waiting for you."

"You thinking about how handsome I am? Charming? Wondering if I'll kiss you again?" Gage teases.

"If you are going to make fun of me you can leave," Zee huffs turning slightly away from the irritating man.

Gage wraps his arms around Zee from behind and rests his cheek next to his. "Don't be like that, babe. You know I like to tease."

Zee bites his lip and tilts his head back to look at Gage. "I know how you can make it up to me…"

Gage smiles and leans in to touch his lips to Zee's.

"And CUT!"

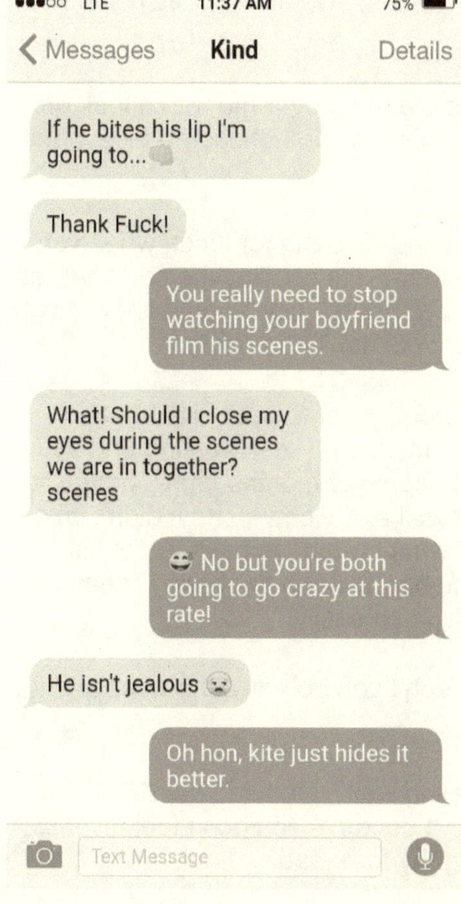


"Let's break for lunch. Filming starts back in two hours."

"You want to have lunch together Kind?" I ask. I am not having lunch with HIM. Not after what he just did.

"I think you have plans, sweetie. I'll catch you both later."

I turn to find Kite standing over me with a look of confusion on his entirely too handsome face. I get up to leave.

"Why are you asking Kind out for lunch when you know we have plans? It's not like she can't eat with us but we have two hours. Don't you want to spend some alone time with me," Kite pouts.

He didn't get to pout. I get to pout. He knows I can't resist his pouty face. After working and dating Kite for the past couple of months I have gotten to know him really well and vice versa. It didn't take him long to find what buttons to push to get his way. Not that he had to push too hard. Today I am not going to give in so easily.

"I'm tired. Why don't you go eat without me and let me go rest?"

"Are you not feeling well? Should I get Billy? Do you need to see a doctor? You don't feel feverish," Kite says feeling my forehead.

Why does he have to be so damn sweet? How can I stay mad at him them? I grab his hand and drag him to an empty corner. Everyone has scattered to go eat lunch, so I'm not worried that anyone will catch us. Even though we haven't told anyone, most of the cast know we are together. They have all been really great about it.

“You called him cute!”

At hearing his laugh I look up and hit him on the chest. That just causes him to laugh harder and pull me into a hug. Kissing the skin below my ear he whispers, “I called a fictional character cute, Cutie. Boss may be handsome but he doesn’t hold a candle to you. I would never call him cutie. That’s my special name for you.”

“You winked at him…”

“Gage winked at Zee.”

“You kissed him,” I mutter pitifully. I know that isn’t fair. But I can’t stop my heart from being jealous and irrational.

“I know. I hate it as much as you do. Don’t think I like it when you have to kiss Fen,” Kite says.

“You never seem to mind,” I accuse.

“I don’t want to make you feel bad, cutie. It’s not easy for me watching the person I love kissing another guy, even when I know it’s for work. I know that you love me Bam and only me. I take comfort in that. I hope you realize that I only love you.”

I bury my face in his chest and hug him tight. “I know. I’m sorry.”

“Feeling possessive, Bam,” Kite smirks.

“Shuddup!” Now I’m embarrassed.

“What! Don’t get shy on me now, cutie. I like it. You feel better now?”

“Yes. I’m starving”

“Let’s go, I can’t let my cutie starve.”

We decide to just see what food service brought in for lunch instead of going out. Kite thinks we can grab some food and then hang out in one of our dressing rooms. I like the plan but it's hard sometimes to dodge our friends.

“There you are. Someone’s been looking for you Bam,” Daw shouts as soon as he sees us. Daw plays Keene’s love interest on the show and I really like him. The two of us have bonded over being newbies to acting. He’s way better at it than I am.

“Bam!”

“Cee?!”

Cebastion or Cee is one of my best friends and one hell of an entertainer. We started out around the same time but Cee is a triple threat. He can sing, dance, and act. I am lucky to have him in my life.

“Bam!” Cee wraps me up in a hug and kisses me full on the lips. Shit! Did Kite just growl?

“Cee, what brings you here?”

Cee lets me go with a pout. "I thought you would be happier to see me."

"I am happy to see you. You just surprised me is all. I thought you were still on tour."

"I am. I have a gap in my schedule and I was asked to play River," Cee exclaims bouncing up and down in excitement.

"You are going to play Nex's ex-boyfriend?" If I remember correctly we are shooting that episode, which is the first episode, starting Monday. "I thought Blake Huntley was playing River."

"I just had them tell you that so I could surprise you. Now let's grab some food and catch up. We haven't seen each other in almost six months. You don't mind if I steal Bam, do you?" Cee asks Kite.

Kite looks between us and I mouth, 'I'm Sorry'.

"Of course not. You two should catch up. I'll go eat with Boss," Kite says with a smirk.

He is so dead teasing me like that.

***

When we are finished filming for the day I pass on having dinner with Cee. It is great to see him but I need to see my guy. I haven't seen HIM since our interrupted lunch attempt and I want to make sure we are okay. You know that saying 'Don't go to bed angry,' well since we don't live together we have promised each other not to part angry.

"Daw, have you seen Kite?"

"I think he might be hanging out with Keene. Can you give me a formal introduction to Cebastion? I'm a huge fan."

"Sure. He will be back on set Monday."

"Thanks Bam! Have a great weekend."

When I reach Keene's dressing room I can hear voices.

"You waiting for Bam?"

"Yeah. You go ahead."

"Okay. I'll see you later at home. Hey Bam, he's waiting for you," Keene greets as he passes me by the door.

"Thanks. Night, Keene."

I walk in and close the door behind me. Kite gestures me over with a crook of his finger. Who knew that move can be so sexy? I'm like a moth drawn to an open flame or a fly caught in a spider's web. Once I am standing in front of him he startles me by pulling me onto his lap.

"Kite!" I scold lightly no heat in my tone. This is a new position for us, me straddling his lap. We haven't went any further than kissing. I think to keep from pouncing on me he always keeps our too short make out sessions fully clothed and upright. I am so ready for more, but I am grateful to have a boyfriend that is understanding and cares about my comfort.

Kite seems to be on a mission as his nose trails along my jaw making me shiver in anticipation of what he is going to do next. I want whatever he has in mind. I want it all with him. I want him. At the feel of hard sucking on my neck I wake from my pleasure fog and push him away. Is he trying to mark me? He knows he can't do that.

"What the hell are you doing? How will I explain a hickey to our director? Kite!" I shout as his hands work their way under my shirt bringing it up and over my head. I stare at him in shock. The look in his eyes is wild, but I'm not afraid. I have never felt more loved than I do right now. Kite brings our lips together for a passionate kiss that sets me on fire. Every nerve ending is tingling and I groan as his hands run down my naked back and squeeze my jean clad ass. Would it be too forward of me to take them off? They are strangling my over excited dick.

"You are mine, Bam. Mine. No one gets to kiss you like this but me. No one gets to touch you like this but me. No one gets to love you like I do but me," Kite murmurs between each kiss.

Catching his face between my palms I make him look at me. "Why are you saying this? You know I'm yours, like you are mine."

“He kissed you, right on the lips like they belonged to him. It couldn’t have been the first time either. You have been kissed before Bam,” Kite growls looking irritated.

I laugh. A full belly laugh shocking my growly bear boyfriend. “Cee and I are just friends. Only friends. Yes, he is very touchy but a brief kiss on the lips as a greeting does not count as a real first kiss! We’re quite the pair, aren’t we? Getting jealous over stupid things,” I say lightly kissing his pouty lips.

“I love you, Bam. I’m afraid you are going to wake up and realize you deserve better,” Kite whispers.

I sigh. My guy had to have been hurt before. Some idiot had to have made him think he wasn’t good enough for him and that is total bullshit. I will spend the rest of my life making sure Kite realizes how special he is.

“Babe, there is no one out there better for me than you. You prove that every single day in the way you treat me and love me. I hope you feel the same about me.”

“I don’t plan on ever letting you go,” Kite promises.

“Good, because I don’t plan on ever letting you go either. Now can we continue what you started?” I ask pushing my still hard cock into his.

“Are you ready for more Bam? I don’t want to rush you if you aren’t?”

See why I love this man so much?

“If you don’t get us naked in the next five minutes I may kill you,” I threaten softly.

“I can do it in three,” Kite smirks.

Best boyfriend ever.

## KITE

I am having a hard time watching Nex and River's break up scene. They are on their fifth take and Bam's tears are real and he is breaking my fucking heart. I just want to yell cut and wrap my cutie up in my arms. Dry away his tears. I am so proud of him right now. He was worried about not being able to pull this scene off and he is killing it. He has some of the crew in tears.

"Cut! I think we have what we need. Great job Bam."

As I make my way over to Bam that friend of his has him in a hug. He really is way too friendly with my cutie, but I trust Bam. Cee is still under review.

"Next time we work together Bam let's make it a comedy. You were breaking my heart, but I'm so glad we got this opportunity."

"Me too, Cee. I think you are leaving with someone's phone number," Bam teases.

Cee smiles looking over at Daw. Huh, maybe I don't have to worry about him after all.

"I'll see you in a couple of weeks for the premiere party. Since it's in LA it coincides with my tour."

"Oh, are you leaving so soon? Don't let the door hit you on the way out," I snark.

“Kite!” Bam scolds.

I’m starting to live to hear him say my name like that.

I shrug not sorry in the least.

“Don’t worry I’m light on feet and the door will never touch my fine ass,” Cee says with a wink. “Take care of my friend or I will be back to kick yours.”

Feisty, I like it. If I ever hurt my cutie no one had to kick my ass, I would kick it myself.

***

Bam has been acting funny. He is hiding something from me and I don’t like it. Tonight is the premiere party for ‘Healing Hearts’. Yes, they decided to change the name of our soap. I’m glad because ‘Too Fab for Words’ just sounded like that Queer Eye for a Straight Guy show. While that show was cool, ours isn’t anything like it. It is hard to believe that eight months have passed. Eight months of getting to know my cutie better. Eight months of falling even deeper in love. My Bam is a thief, stealing my heart, but the truth is I willingly gave it to him long ago.

We have a month of downtime before we start filming again, if we get picked up for another season. Since Bam didn’t get a chance for a vacation between his tour and filming I am surprising him with a vacation, after we visit his family and mine. I won’t lie, I am scared shitless to meet his family. Both our families know but actually having the meet and greet is something entirely different than talking on the phone.

"You ready, Kite?"

I hope that no matter how long we are together he will always make my heart race and my breath catch. He looks stunning to me all the time in no matter what he wears, but right now dressed in an all-black suit he is breathtaking and I would like nothing more than to stay home and keep in in bed.

"Don't give me that look mister! We have to go," Bam say wagging a finger at me. My cutie knows me so well.

"You look amazing cutie. Yes, I'm ready. Let's go wow everyone with our new show."

Bam takes my hand and giggles. It's a beautiful sound.

"Thank you all for coming to our special viewing of the first episode of 'Healing Hearts'. I would like to introduce our cast and then we have some surprise performance for you. Please enjoy."

After an hour of mingling and eating delicious food I am wondering where my cutie has gotten to. We got separated somewhere between the fun little mini tacos and the decadent cheesecake. Mmm, I wonder if they have any more of that cheesecake.

I look towards the stage as I hear a sweet melody start playing. I smile to see Bam sitting on a stool playing his guitar.

"When I started this project I didn't realize at the time that it was going to change my life."

Is he going to do what I think he's going to do?

"Nex and I are very similar. We are both pop singers, shy, and have great friends."

Cutie, are you going to out yourself in front of all of these people? I'm thrilled, but you don't have to do this.

"Nex and I are both gay."

I can hear a shocked awe go through the crowd and low murmurs kick up. Bam is staring right at me as he says each word and I know I'm not breathing. He looks so brave and I am so proud of him.

"How Nex and I differ is that I had never been in love before until now. I am not stepping out of the closet now because I am in love, but because it is the right time to do it. While Nex went through a journey of discovery and falling in love so did I. I have never been ashamed or tried to hide my sexuality, but it really wasn't anyone's business when I was a teenager. It still really isn't anyone's business but I want to be free to hold my boyfriend's hand who I can see I have shocked with my little confession tonight. I know I have been acting out of sorts these past few weeks and this is why."

I step up closer to the stage so I can see his face clearer.

"Thank you for loving me, Kite. For letting go of all of the reasons we shouldn't work and taking a chance on something special. You have changed my life for the better and I look forward to what our future brings. This song is sung from Nex to Ollie, but I wrote it for you. I love you."

I'm not crying…

Dammit, I need a tissue...and this is before I hear the song.

*Falling, falling, falling, for you*
*Might be the last thing I do*
*There may be a million reasons*
*why*
*Why it won't last*

*Falling, falling, falling for you*
*My heart won't ever feel the same*
*Staking its claim*
*My life will never ever be the*
*same*

*Can't catch my breath*
*My heart can't be denied*
*You push, I pull*

*Falling, falling, falling for you….*

I don't hear the rest as I push my way through the crowd trying to make it to the back of the stage. I want to, no I NEED to touch him as soon as possible. I'm there as he is taking his last bow and turning to walk backstage. When he sees me he runs and I pick him up lifting his feet off the ground.

"You didn't have to do that," I breathed into his skin.

"I know. I wanted to. No hiding, Kite. I want the world to know you are mine."

I kiss him, my heart near bursting. I don't deserve this beautiful man, but he is mine and I'm his and that is all I need.

## EPILOGUE

## BARAMEE

I glance at my phone and see that it's Billy calling. I answer it because I know that if I don't he will just keep calling until I do.

"I have one more week of vacation. Why are you bothering me?" I demand. Traveling with Kite for the past three weeks has been heaven. At this very moment Billy is interrupting cuddle time if you know what I mean.

"I just wanted to call and give you the good news."

Kite is being naughty trying to distract me with wandering hands and lips. I will not moan while I am on the phone with my manager. I slap Kite on the head and he just grins at me unrepentant. How did I get so lucky to call this man mine? Shit, what is he saying?

"Bam, are you listening?"

No, it's a little hard too when you have a hot and sexy boyfriend teasing you.

"What...Mmmm?" Crap! That was a moan.

"What are you doing? You know what never mind. 'Healing Hearts' ratings are through the roof and the network has renewed it for three more seasons. People are loving it Bam. Filming starts in a week. You hear that Kite!"

"Yes, Billy. We will be back in a week. That is probably Malik calling on the other line."

"See you in a week, kid. Stay out of trouble."

"Always, Billy." Kite ends the call and shuts the phone off throwing it on the floor. "Aren't you going to talk to Malik?"

"No, cutie. He can wait. You on the other hand…"

Best Boyfriend Ever!

The Shorty Collection: Love Stories in Various Lengths

# TWO HANDS COLLIDED

***Two hands collided reaching for a book on the top shelf in the fiction area of the library.***

A small hand quickly grabbed a hold of the spine and snatched the book away from me pulling it down to a hoodie covered chest. I let out a loud snort, not believing someone could be so rude. Looking the kid up and down my amused gaze locked onto a pair of dark eyes. They were like gazing into a stormy night.

Girls had to be jealous over his long lashes. Perfectly curled at the tips and black as midnight. Every time he blinked they kissed the tops of his cheeks. It was all in HI-Def due to the round plastic frame glasses perched on his button nose.

A clearing of a throat brought me out of my day dreaming. Re-focusing, I chuckled softly at the disgruntled look on Specs face. The look the little dude was throwing me was fierce, he was not about to give up his prize.

“Since you already have three books, it only seems fair that you let me have that one,” I reasoned.

“Sorry, I touched it first. First come, first serve.”

Everything about that statement was wrong. Conjured all sorts of naughty scenarios in my mind.

“If you want to read it I'll be returning it on Friday.”

I scoffed. “Friday! This Friday? As in the Friday that is two days from now!”

“Yes, captain obvious.” Specs growled and turned to head to the circulation counter.

“Hey! Wait a fucking minute. No way can you read four door stoppers in two days,” I argued. All those books Specs had in his arms had to be over four hundred pages. I was surprised the little guy hadn't been crushed by the weight.

“I so fucking can. Not that I have to prove anything to you.” I could see that Specs was getting annoyed. I watched as he all but threw the books on the counter for the girl to check out.

“You don't have to be rude. Didn't your mother teach you to be respectful to your elders?” I asked starting to get pissed off myself. Who did this little shit think he was? Sure he was cute as fuck but that didn't give him the right to be a prick.

I gaped at him as he laughed. Not just a giggle or a chuckle, but a full out belly laugh like what I had said was funny as hell.

Picking up his books Specs looked me in the eye and smiled. "Wilder, I'm four days older than you asshole."

"See you Friday, Enzo," the girl gave him a wave and Enzo smirked at me. I stood there stunned.

Enzo Wietzman.

Once upon a time we had been neighbors.

Once upon a time Enzo and I had taken baths together. My mom would break out those pics every now and then just to make me blush.

Once upon a time we had been inseparable...until his family moved away.

It looked like Enzo Wietzman had moved home.

***Two hands collided over the last slice of pepperoni pizza in the busy cafeteria line.***

This time I was faster, snatching that square piece of heaven right out from under my short stuff's nose.

"Too slow, small fry," I crowed. Sure, I sounded like a baby but I felt victorious.

"Whatever," Enzo mumbled grabbing a bowl of mac and cheese.

As we paid for our food a ton of questions swirled through my head, but I only cared about one.

Did you miss me like I missed you?

Enzo had disappeared from my life when we were 12. At that age it was hard to keep in touch. I had thought we would be best friends forever. It had ended up being a childish dream.

"I stopped by the library Friday and sure enough that book had been returned," I said instead of what was really on my mind.

Who was your first date? Did you enjoy your first kiss?

"I told you it would be." Enzo snapped. He still was short tempered.

"I still don't think you read all four books," I goaded. If Enzo was anything like he had been when we were kids, I know he had. I wanted to tease him, like I used to. Enzo wouldn't so much blush as turn a bright shade of red in anger. He looked good angry.

Enzo took a seat at the table next to where I sat with my friends, but I wasn't about to be ignored. I took the seat opposite him so I could stare at him.

"So, you like me, huh?"

My heart stuttered to a stop.

Enzo continued talking oblivious to my heart condition, "I do like you. I like you a lot. How do you feel about me?"

How do I feel about you? I've loved you since we were five.

"I just met you. How do you know you like me?"

Wait, just met me? What the hell? Now he was losing me...

"I just do. It might not make sense to anyone else and it might seem a bit crazy, but I fell for you the moment we met and each moment since keeps telling me I'm right."

Fuck me. He was quoting that book we had both wanted, The Heart of the Melody by Jae Le. I wasn't quite finished with it but I had read the passage he was referring too.

"Stop," I croaked. I had forgotten how good Enzo was at turning the tables on me. Enzo got up from the table leaving his food uneaten. Stepping up close to me he leaned in to whisper in my ear, making a shiver roll up my spine.

"I missed you, Wild."

I swore I could still feel Enzo's lips on the shell of my ear for the remainder of the day.

***Two hands collided pushing the restaurant door open on Saturday morning.***

I already knew who the hand belonged to without even looking up to see the owner's face. Wilder's hands hadn't changed much since we were kids, just had gotten bigger.

"Short stuff, fancy meeting you here."

Same old Wild. His nicknames for me hadn't changed either.

"I'm meeting a couple friends here for breakfast before we head to the library to work on a project." I wasn't sure why I felt the need to explain, but with Wilder I always seemed to need to.

Wilder and I had our first playdate when we were 3. It ended in tears when he took the Tonka Truck I was playing with and I pinched him. Our relationship wasn't much different after that. I wasn't shy, but I enjoyed reading and spending time on my own. Wilder liked being around people and was always looking for adventure. At least I could read in detention.

"Can I sit with you while you wait? I'm just getting a to go," Wilder asked.

"Sure."

I knew he would grow up to be gorgeous. His shock of white blonde hair fell in waves over his forehead into his electric blue eyes. When he smiled that dimple of his deepened. I wanted to kiss it.

"I'll just have a coffee for right now. I'm waiting for my friends." I told the waitress.

"Bacon cheeseburger with fries."

"For breakfast, Wild?" I arched my brow and scrunched up my nose.

"Yes, Enzo. Don't you remember we used to eat them all the time at my Grandma's? No one could grill like Nana," Wild said with a laugh.

Yeah I remembered. I remembered everything. I remembered the way you hugged me the day I moved away. The way your heart beat against mine. The smell of your shampoo. Most importantly how tight you held me. I loved you even then.

As I let you go that last time my heart was equal parts devastated and relieved. Devastated to be leaving my best friend and most likely never seeing you again. Also relieved to be leaving my best friend who I loved way more than a friend. I knew you would never feel the same way.

"What made you move back? Not that I'm not glad to see you. Just surprised me seeing you in the library."

“Parents got divorced. Mom wanted to move home.” I added cream and sugar to my coffee thinking about how happy I was my parents finally decided to give it up. They just weren't good for each other. I had been ecstatic to find out Mom had wanted to move back here. Running into Wild at the library a few days before school had started had been perfect.

“I am glad you are back Enzo,” Wild said as his to go bag was placed at the table.

Did you miss me, Wild? Did you miss me like I missed you?

Getting up from the table Wild leaned in close to my ear, similar to what I had did to him the other day, making a shiver sweep over my body.

“I missed you, Zo. A lot.”

The grin that spread across my face was as stupid as his had been.

***Two hands collided as term papers were turned in to the teacher on the way out of the classroom.***

"You can't seem to keep your hands to yourself. Can you Wilder?" I smirked.

"You want me to, short stuff," Wilder answered with a shit eating grin.

No, I did not.

"You and your mom are still coming over for dinner, right?" Wider asked.

"Yes. We will see you at seven."

"Awesome, see you later Zo."

After dinner our parents shooed us away. We were a little old to be going out to play but taking a walk to the park in Wild's neighborhood, my old neighborhood, sounded like a good idea.

Walking over to the shady tree behind the swing set I started hunting for something.

"What are you doing?" Wild asked curiously.

"I know it's around here somewhere. There!"

EW + WR = BFF

“Wow. I had forgotten we had did this,” Wilder said in awe.

“We were ten. You were wearing that football jersey you loved so much and a baseball cap. I remembered thinking, “Should I think my male best friend looks cute.”

“Enzo…”

“I stopped sleeping over at your house because I was afraid you would catch me staring at you. I thought you were the most beautiful person. It killed me to move away from you Wild, but it would have killed me more to find out you didn’t like me the way I liked you.”

“Enzo…”

“We go off to college in a few months and I don’t want to go another five years without telling you how I feel about you.” I couldn't look at him. I was too afraid he would look disgusted, and too hopeful he wouldn’t.

“Enzo...fucking look at me,” Wilder growled.

Startled, I raised my eyes to look him dead on. It wasn’t disgust etched on his handsome features, but love.

Grabbing me by the collar he drew me flush against his body, so our lips were mere inches apart..

"You talk too damn much," Wilder muttered as his lips captured mine causing a fire to heat in my belly. My eyes slid shut and my hands fisted in his t-shirt as our tongues tasted each other for the first time. I was so fucking ruined for any other guy. Wilder fucking ruined me.

"I have wanted to kiss you since you stole that book from me in the library," Wilder confessed once he released me from his kiss and pressed his forehead to mine.

"Why didn't you?" I teased.

"I didn't want to get book slapped. Those damn books you read are fucking weapons, Zo," Wilder said laughing.

"They can come in handy."

"I never would have rejected you. I have always felt the same as you. You broke my heart moving away. I felt it beat again after our hands collided that first time. It has been beating ever since."

I smiled at the boy I had loved forever, "I purpose that we keep our hands colliding."

"For a long, long time."

***Two hands collided and laced together.....their heartbeats playing their own love song.***

# TOGETHER

“Let's break up.”

“Hmm…did you want soda or milk to go with dinner?”

“Let's break up.”

“Stop messing around and come eat. I'll get you some tea.”

“Let's break up.”

Slamming the glass on the table I turn to glare at my lover. “No! I said stop talking nonsense and come eat before the food gets cold.”

We aren't breaking up. Arranging the rest of the food on the table I sit down to eat. I'm not letting this ridiculous conversation ruin my appetite.

Across from me the food starts disappearing with steady speed.

“Let's break up.” is whispered after the last bite is chewed and swallowed.

“No.”

I grab the now empty plates and head to the sink. I am not going to be cast aside so easily. I, we, have over ten years invested in this relationship. I am not going away without a fight.

“Don't be so stubborn. Let's break up!”

“Give me one good reason why?”

“I don't love you.”

Even though I know it is a fucking lie, hearing it out loud makes my heart twist.

“Liar.”

“Don't confuse sex for love,” comes the rough reply.

Asshole. I can feel every kiss, caress, embrace from our love making the night before. Parts of me still tingle and now I'm having to listen to vicious lies.

“Try again.”

Blue eyes blaze my way in anger. Beautiful blue eyes I love so much. “I'm done talking. I don't want to be with you anymore.”

Snatching his wrist as he tries to pass I bring him tight into my embrace.

“That's too fucking bad because you took a vow…”

"Fuck you, Ace! Fuck you. You know why I'm trying to do this. Just let me go. Please."

"Why are you making me let you go before I have to? The doctors said you have a fifty fifty chance and I plan on fighting. Are you just planning on dying?"

From the way he isn't looking at me that's exactly what he is planning.

"Cole Daton, we are married and that means for better or for worse and in sickness and in health. Would you expect me to leave if I had been diagnosed with cancer? Or would you have left me?"

He looks horrified. "No! I love you. You know that, but I don't want you to see me die. I watched my father die from this same fucking disease and it was devastating. Will you please let me spare you that?"

"No. Please don't deny me being with you, loving you and taking care of you when you need it most. I'm your husband. You are my family, my lover, my heart. I'm begging you Cole, don't shut me out."

I can feel his tears against my shoulder. "I'm scared."

Kissing his temple I rock us in place. "I know, baby. Isn't it better to be scared together? Then to be scared all alone. Like we have gotten through everything since we were seventeen, we will get through this together."

Finally a smile breaks out on his handsome face.

"Yes, Ace. Together."

# TOASTED

"Let's hear it for Luanne. Beautiful, isn't she…" Ozzy hated open mic night the most out of all the theme nights this damn bar hosted once a week. Luanne thought herself to be Madonna, while she sounded like a cat in heat. Of all the damn days to forget his ear plugs. "Up next we have a newcomer taking the stage here at Toasted. Let's give a warm welcome to Cril." He hopes like hell he doesn't make his ears bleed.

As Ozzy makes his way back to the bar he picks up the empties and mentally files away the orders being shouted his way. He does have to give himself a pat on the back. These open mic nights, however cringe inducing they are, keep his bar packed every Wednesday night. Dropping the dirty ones in the wash bin Ozzy goes about making those drink orders. Seeing Missy he flags her down to come pick them up.

"Uh...hi...I'm Cril, and I hope you like my music."

Taking a moment to glance up from the beer in his hand he finds himself transfixed. The kid is beautiful. Ozzy will admit he wasn't paying a lot of attention while he was introducing him, but he knows he would remember someone as stunning as him if I had seen him before. Dark black hair, pale creamy skin, and his voice... His voice is giving him...well he's not going to mention what Cril's voice is doing to him.

"Boss!"

Shit! The beer was overflowing and he didn't even feel it cooling his fingers. "Sorry! Let me pour a new one and the rest are for tables 5, 7, and 8."

Missy rolls her eyes at him and takes the tray once he has properly poured the remaining glass. He's used to Missy laughing at him so he smiles. It has been awhile since a guy has turned his head.

***

"I have no interest in going to a bar tonight."

"That's because you have no interest in having fun," Pim groans. "I'm not letting you spend your twenty-first birthday at home playing video games Shu."

"I'd just give in now, dude. You know how she can be. Ow." Andy grins sheepishly as he rubs his head. "I love you, baby."

Pim shushes him and continues glaring at Shu. He knows this look well. She has been throwing that look at him since they were four, and she knows he can't resist the look.

**20 minutes later**

"Isn't this fun?!" Pim shouts over the Madonna wannabe.

More like fucking torture. "Fun," I say in a mocking tone. "I'm going to get a drink with my legal self."

"Shu!"

He loves Pim. He really does. But ever since he broke up with his boyfriend a couple months ago she has made it her mission to bring him out of his funk. He hasn't been in a funk. The breakup was mutual and Shu's not even sad about it. They just weren't meant to be. But who is at twenty.

"Happy Birthday! Is this your first official drink as the big 2-1?"

"Yep, thanks." Shu takes the beer from the bartender and his breath catches as their fingers brush. If he has been affected by the touch Shu can't tell, but his own fingers are still tingling. Shu knows he's staring.

"This one's on me. No birthday is complete without your birthday smacks."

Shu's eyes grow big. Smacks? What the hell? He just met this man. It doesn't matter how hot he finds him. Leaning over the bar he takes Shu's face between his hands and proceeds to give each cheek ten loud smacks with his lips.

"And Twenty-One." The last one lands right on Shu's stunned lips.

Fuck...he should not be turned on right now.

"Happy Birthday, Shu. I have to go and introduce the next act."

Well, hell...he knows Shu's name but what's his?

***

Don't be nervous, don't be nervous, don't be nervous….

Cril really hates his friends right now.

***"Come on Cril you have to try it."***

***"You are so talented."***

***"Chicken."***

Fucking, Tank. Cril will kill him first. Tank knows Cril has stage fright.

"Uh...hi...I'm Cril, and I hope you like my music."

Great, he sounds like an idiot. *Just picture everyone naked and pretend like you are singing in the shower.* Opening his eyes he's staring at a guy he's seen at school. Cril can't remember his name but he has a nice smile. He's smiling at him right now. He can do this.

After his three song time limit is over he's overwhelmed to see the whole place up on their feet clapping and screaming. His heart is beating so fast right now.

"Thank you...so much."

"Wow! I think I speak for the whole crowd when I say you were fantastic!" the bar owner says after joining me on the stage.

Cril knows he's grinning like a fool. "Thank you."

"Please come back and play, anytime." Is that interest Cril sees in his eyes? No way. No way would he be interested in him. As he removes his hand Cril's left with his card. "Open mic might be over for tonight but the night is still young. Last call isn't for two more hours. Enjoy the rest of the evening."

Cril follows him off the stage and blurts out, "Are you hitting on me?"

Turning he smiles, taking Cril off guard. What is up with this stupid heart of his? It gets excited first over that school guys smile and now his. Cool it!

"Do you want me to be hitting on you?"

Gripping his guitar he can feel his cheeks burning. Fucking light skin.

"You are too fucking cute."

“Excuse me, we go to school together, don’t we?”

Taking his eyes off the smirking jerk Cril focuses on his classmate. “Yes, but I don’t think we are in any classes together.”

“I just wanted to tell you I really enjoyed your music. I’m Shu, by the way.”

“Ozzy,” the smirking hot jerk pipes up. “You know what? This is perfect. Shu is celebrating a birthday and it is only right that we help him.”

Both Shu and Cril look at Ozzy like he’s grown a second head. Ozzy’s easy going nature is hard to resist and minutes later Cril finds himself walking towards the arcade with Ozzy to the left of him and Shu on the right. How did this even happen?

***

*Ok, Ozzy what the hell are you doing?* While it isn’t unlike him to leave closing the bar up to Missy it is unlike him to practically kidnap not one, but two barely legal boys. He knows that Cril can’t be 21. Having had worked in restaurants since he was sixteen and then buying this bar after graduating college he’s a pretty good judge of someone's age.
Since his bar serves food and has a seperate area for dining it is also open to families. At twenty eight Ozzy’s not ancient but watching Cril and Shu play the arcade games is making him feel his age.

He hasn’t been in a relationship in a while. No, please don’t ask how long a while is. You’re getting awfully personal! Anyway, he’s surprised that he’s not only feeling a stirring for Cril but for Shu as well. He isn't the only one that felt something when his and Shu's fingers touched. Ozzt never should have kissed Shu. That had been a damn fool thing to do. He's not one to believe in love at first sight. Lust, hell yes. Like, sure. But love, he does think that takes time. He's supposed to love one at a time. Not two.

***

"Is it really your birthday today?" Cril asks.

"Yep."

"Happy Birthday. I turned nineteen a couple weeks ago. I'm a freshman. You're a junior, right?"

Shu nods his head. He's trying to figure out where he's seen Cril before when it hits him. "Third floor showers."

Cril's cheeks pink up and he has to agree with Ozzy. He is fucking adorable. "What?"

"I hear you singing in the third floor shower room. I've never seen your face before. Are you majoring in music?"

"No, business. Music is a hobby."

"You're damn good at it."

"Thank you. I've seen you play basketball. You're really good too."

"It's a good workout. What do you think he has in mind?" Shu asks, eyeing Ozzy sitting on the bench watching us.

"Not sure but he's hot as fuck," Cril blurts out immediately looking embarrassed.

"I agree. So are you," Shu says, looking at Cril dead on.

"Wha...at?" He's really cute when he stutters.

"I think Ozzy thinks the same."

"I do think the same. About both of you, actually," Ozzy says quietly. "Not exactly sure what it means."

"Maybe it just means that we would like to get to know each other better," Cril suggests. "I know I would like that a lot."

At the beginning of the evening Shu was single, now towards the end he potentially has two dates. This was turning out to be a fantastic birthday. He may even thank Pim.

***

"Did you ever thank Pim for dragging you to Toasted that night?" Cril asks Shu as he and I get wrapped up in our Ozzy's arms, hearts slowly beating normally again after our 'workout'. Use your imaginations, you dirty minded people.

"Uh, I think I might have once Pim got over the shock of her best friend falling in love with two men." Shu gives each of them a kiss. Falling in love is a beautiful thing when you meet the right person. Cril just happened to have met the two right persons. It has been a beautiful thing, with a few twists and turns along their path.

To all their haters, they say fuck you. They don't need anyone's approval.

Their personalities complement each other. Ozzy is a big, huge lovable goofball. He is also a businessman who knows how to take care of his shit. It's not just his good looks that makes him attractive, but the way he is responsible and how he loves and takes care of Cril and Shu. Shu is actually really quiet and reserved. Give that boy a Gameboy and you have given him the greatest treasure. Shu has the biggest heart and he will take care of everyone around him before he takes care of himself. As for Cril, he's lucky to have them. He can be a brat. He likes to get his way, sulk, and be cherished. He cherishes them even more.

"It's okay,I personally thanked Pim and your friends for making you come out for open mic night," Ozzy sighs. "Best night of my life."

"I guess that just leaves me and Shu to thank you for being a perv and hitting on young boys," Cril teases.

"Don't be mean to our old man now, Cril. He needs time to rest and recuperate before we can properly thank him. He isn't young and virile anymore," Shu goads with a raised brow.

The look on Ozzy's face is priceless and they don't render him speechless often.

"Old...man?? I'll show you an old man. Let's see if you are still sassy when I'm done with you."

# PERFECT KISSES

## SEVEN

From a young age I could be found with my body bent contentedly over a sketchbook, hand flying over the page trying to get the image out of my head and onto the page as fast as I could. Those first few books looked messy and incomplete, but my mother still had them displayed proudly on her bookshelf. A few of her favorites were torn out and framed on her wall. As I grew older and started to learn my passion my hand slowed down taking care in every stroke of the pencil, pen, paint brush, I decided to wield that day. Every sketch, drawing, painting had a story. As the storyteller I had a duty to bring each unique one to life.

Every story has a beginning. I know you have heard Once Upon a Time a million times before. Some of our favorite fairy tales begin with those four simple words. Some people use another classic, I Remember When. My story starts with a kiss. A perfect first kiss that spiraled over the years into countless perfect kisses. It is all the fault of one man.

## ***First Kiss***

*By our third date I knew you were the one and we hadn't even kissed yet. I loved the way you talked, laughed, the way your hair was always in your eyes. You always got so nervous when our bodies would get too close. I found that so fucking adorable and still do. I've never to this day seen another man as beautiful as you. I call you beautiful just to see that look in your eye. That little spark of fire. It usually leads to delicious...things. Anyway I'm getting ahead of myself. Our first kiss was on that third date. Do you remember? You were so nervous. I watched as you rocked from foot to foot. I wanted to put you out of your misery and kiss you first but I waited because I knew it would be that much sweeter coming from you. That first taste, yet all too brief, was So sweet. I was a goner.*

*Our noses smushed.*
*Our teeth clicked.*
*You stepped on my toes.*

*But that first taste of your soft lips made me weak in the knees.*

*It was perfect.*

I feel someone peering over my shoulder and I turn to him with a smile.

“Why are you frowning?”

“I don’t remember our first kiss being quite like that.”

I love when my Wyette pouts.

“How do you remember it?”

“I did not step on your toes.”

“But you don’t deny the nose smushing or nearly breaking my tooth,” I tease.

“Seven!”

As he turns to walk away in a huff I stop him with a wrist grab. I know it’s cliché but it really is damn sexy and I pull him onto my lap. With practiced ease our lips collide in a heated kiss. The type of kiss that will lead us straight to the bedroom. It’s another perfect kiss.

## WYETTE

Slipping out of our warm bed I leave my stunning artist to sleep a few more hours. I'm curious to see what he is working on. He has been mum lately and I only got a little peek earlier. Powering the computer back on, I take a look at the open sketch book before me. My eyes tear up. The first sketch I see is of our first kiss. It really was the way he described it.

I met Seven in college. I was a senior ready to graduate and he was a few years older doing a guest lecture for one of my art classes. My Seven is a successful artist. Owns his own gallery. I'm a librarian at the Art Institute. We really are one of those gag me with a spoon couples. After ten years together we are still very much in love. I even want to gag just saying that. We aren't perfect. No couple is. We fight over stupid shit. He leaves his clothes laying all over the fucking place. Never puts his dirty dishes in the sink. How hard is it to put the cap back on the toothpaste?

When we kiss...I won't say it's like the first time because that was innocent and shy. Sweet and nerve wracking. Perfect, in its blushes of falling in love. Our kisses have evolved, grown. They are just more. More passionate, filled with love, hungry, even sweeter. Each one we have shared is more perfect than the last. Seven has talked about writing our love story for a while now. This way, through our kisses, is perfect.

## *Fifth Kiss*

*Some would say that I couldn't possibly remember our fifth kiss, but I would tell those some they are wrong. Right after our first kiss we had our second. The first had been so brief. I will admit I don't recall the third and fourth in vivid detail but the fifth...well the fifth had led to other things. Seven hadn't been my first boyfriend and I wasn't his but he was the first to make me really want to see what all my friends had been talking about. I wasn't a virgin but they talked like sex was this out of body experience that was better than chocolate. Between you and me none of my previous boyfriends had been better than chocolate. Our fifth kiss had been on his couch in his tiny studio apartment. He had invited me over for dinner. Dessert had been ice cream.*

*Ice cream smudged mouth.*
*Warm hand on the nape of my neck.*
*Even warmer tongue licking the smudge away.*
*Seven got creative with the rest of the melting ice cream and my very naked body. I did mention he's an artist right?*

*Chocolate isn't my favorite anymore. Seven is. Everything about that night was perfect.*

"You peeked. This is supposed to be my anniversary gift to you."

"It's beautiful. I wrote my version of kiss number five. I hope you don't mind," I say, biting my lip.

Seven just smiles and sits in my lap.

"Of course not. This story is as much yours as it is mine. Did you look at the picture?"

"No, you already drew our fifth kiss?" I start flipping the pages and I stop when I find the one of us sitting on the couch. My lips are tinted with ice cream and my eyes have a hooded, sexy look. Seven is leaning in, but hasn't quite bridged the gap. I swear I can see the tip of his tongue sticking out ready to lick the ice cream up.

"If you want me again tonight it's my turn to lead," Seven whispers, making me shiver.

"Deal. But no more going down memory lane tonight. I don't think either of our asses will appreciate it."

Seven laughs and I push him up off my lap taking his hand so he can lead me into our bedroom. I'm looking forward to revisiting those memories again tomorrow.

Sunday afternoons. I countdown the days, hours, minutes until it is Sunday afternoon once again. I can hear Seven squirming on the chair behind me and I softly chuckle to myself. How many Sunday's has it been now that we have spent like this? Do you get tired of them? Because I know I never will. I straighten from my bent position at the oven holding a piping hot pan of banana bread loaves. Seven groans. Partly from the delicious smell that has permeated the room and partly from ruining his view of my fine assets. I wore these faded, low rise jeans he loves and a tight grey tee that has been washed so many times it is soft like butter. I'm not evil. I'm a tease. I sit a plate of bread on the table with butter and chocolate hazelnut spread next to it.

"Milk?"

"Coffee."

"What kiss is up next?" I ask, as I busy myself preparing his coffee the way he likes it. Two creams, and two sugars. Me...I like it blonde. Just add a little coffee to my cream.

"That kiss where you threw a tantrum in front of everyone."

His coffee cup hits the table with more force than is necessary and hot liquid splashes on my fingers.

"Babe! Are you okay?" Seven reaches for my hand bringing my reddening digits to his mouth to blow on. Giving them a kiss I glared at his smile.

"Tantrum? Me!?"

Seven winks and shows me his sketch pad. I huff out a breath in annoyance at being teased and hit him with my elbow. Just seeing his drawing brings it all back.

## Tantrum Kiss

*I know what my Seven will say. It isn't possible to keep track of kisses by number once you have made love. I'm inclined to agree. Our first kiss started it all. The fifth kiss introduced me to the joys of sex. Sex, well Seven and I kiss a lot during sex so I have lost count of our kisses after number five. It's sort of like that Owl asking how many licks does it take to get to the center of a Tootsie pop? It took him three but in our ten years together I'm sure we have shared tens of thousands of kisses and thousands of those were probably while we were getting down and dirty. But there are those kisses that stand out. Are special.*

*While in college to make extra money I would do odd jobs at an art studio. One of those jobs was posing nude. Seven isn't the first guy to call me beautiful and I'm not ashamed of my body. It was always a professional environment and the pay was good. After Seven and I had been together for about three months I'd been called to pose for a class. I didn't know that Seven was the teacher. Imagine both of our surprises. My Seven isn't known for his punctuality so as usual he was running late. The assistant told me to disrobe and the students could get started without him.*

*Have you seen an artist throw a tantrum? It was impressive, especially in two different languages.*

*Possessive hands hauling my body to his.*
*Demanding mouth devouring mine.*
*So fucking turned on.*

*"No one sees you like this but me. You're in so much fucking trouble."*

*When he felt what was hard and insistent against his thigh he groaned and growled, "You ARE so much fucking trouble, but I love you. Everyone get out! Leave your drawings. Now!"*

*That was my last paid nudie job. That kiss had been epic.*

## SEVEN

On our tenth wedding anniversary Wyette and I sit on our couch with a beautifully bound book balancing on our knees between us.

Ten Years of Perfect Kisses
Written by Seven and Wyette
Artwork by Seven

Over glasses of wine and small bites of cheesecake we slowly turn the pages savoring each story. Our perfect kisses: First, fifth, tantrum, graduation, engagement, wedding, buying a house, adopting a dog; tells our love story.

"Should we make a new memory?" Wyette asks, as we close the book. "One to add to our next book?"

I don't answer with words. I let my lips speak for me.

# SANTA BABY

"Do I look like a Santa to you?"

Standing in only a pair of tight red boxer briefs Kale patted his abs and gave his boyfriend a questioning look.

No, Core thought, his man did not resemble the jolly fat man but that's what those red suits were for.

"My sister has a suit for you and some stuffing. Plus a beard."

"Forget it. You do it," Kale grumbled.

"Baby, you are better with kids than I am. Piper is going to pay you $200 for each event and she has ten booked for the rest of the year. Plus you know we can use the money," Core smiled making sure his dimple popped. Kale was a sucker for the dimple.

"That explains him but what the hell about me!"

Both men turned to look in the direction of the petulant voice.

Bing tapped his foot a mile a minute in irritation, causing the jingle ball on the elf shoe he was wearing to make it sound like the start of jingle bells.

How did he even end up in this monstrosity? Tights! Core tricked him into a pair of candy cane striped tights! Along with the tights the outfit was rounded off with knee length green elf pants, a white long sleeve shirt, and suspenders. If he clutched the headband with the pointy ears in his hands any harder they were going to snap in half.

"Bingy! Santa needs a helper."

"Great, you do it asshole," Bing yelled.

"I'm the photographer. You look ador…"

"If you say adorable, Core, you can kiss ever getting another blow job from me goodbye until next year." Seeing the amused look on Kale's face Bing pointed at him, "You think of laughing and you won't get your dick near my sweet ass until your birthday."

"Bing!"

"Bingy!"

It was only the beginning of December and Kale's birthday was next June. Their Bing was vicious and he was usually true to his word.

“Piper is going to pay you $100. It's for an hour, two hours tops. Please, baby. You know we can use the money,” Core cajoled in a sweet voice.

“Fine. But you owe us, Core.”

Core nodded his head up and down in agreement.

“What can I do right now to make it up to you?” said question was asked with a head tilt and a lick to his lower lip.

“Right now?” Bing threw the offensive elf ears on the dresser and toed the idiotic shoes off flinging them into the corner. “You can get me out of these ridiculous clothes.”

“Bing.”

Bing jolted in surprise as Kale wrapped an arm around his waist and hot breath ghosted over his ear making him shiver. When had Kale even moved?

“As punishment Core will sit in that chair and watch as I reveal your delicious skin bit by bit. While I get to touch and taste, he has to sit on his hands and try not to drool on himself,” Kale proposed gleefully, nuzzling Bings neck.

“I can't even touch myself!” Core whined in outrage.

“Nope, now be a good boy and go sit down.”

Core made a show of being upset, but they all knew nothing turned him on more than watching his guys tease him. Kale waited until Core was seated with his hands under him before he proceeded. Bing was already shaking slightly in anticipation. Before Core had sprung the news on them that Piper needed help for her party planning business, they had planned a lazy day in watching movies, eating take out, and making love. It was a rare occasion when all three had a day off together. The life of a working college student was a busy one and none of their schedules were the same.

Bing was the only one fully dressed in the elf costume, which he did look fucking adorable in. But Kale would never say that to his Bingy's face. He liked his balls right where they were. They weren't kidding when they said he had a vicious streak. Even that was fucking cute.

Running his hands up Bings chest Kale pushed the suspenders off his shoulders. All eyes were on Core as each button of the white shirt was undone revealing glimpses of Bings creamy white skin.

With a shrug the shirt slid down and Kale helped Bing get it off his wrists letting it fall to the floor. Bing having had it with the pants and tights roughly pushed them off his hips and stomped them off once they were by his feet. That left him in nothing but what he started off in that morning, light blue boxers.

"Our Bingy is beautiful like this, isn't he…"

"Yes." Core's voice was ragged. Bing didn't like it when they called him adorable, cute, or beautiful but he was to them. Especially when his skin was flushed a dusty rose. His eyes were glazed in passion. His obvious arousal was making a wet spot through his briefs. Just showed how much he wanted them. "Now make him moan, Kale."

"Fuck..." Bing let out on a shaky breath. "You're not playing fair."

"When have we ever?" Kale whispered before capturing Bings lips sliding his tongue along the crease seeking entrance. On a sigh Bing welcomed the languid meeting of tongues and slight nips of teeth.

Moans and whimpers were coaxed out of Bing with every mind numbing suck to the tender skin of his neck, pinch to his hard nipples, and caress of his cute little Buddha belly. Bing didn't like how fascinated him and Core were with his belly, but they couldn't get enough of it. When he felt Bings legs start to give Kale caught him around the waist.

"Am I making you weak in the knees, baby?" Kale teased.

"Way to state the obvious, asshole," Bing muttered between pants.

"You're losing your touch Kale. He's still able to smartass."

Kale chuckled and whispered in Bing's ear, "Am I not enough to silence the smartass, baby? You want Core too?"

"I always want you and Core, both. Always."

"We know, baby, we know." Kale picked Bing up gesturing for Core to go to the bed.

As soon as Bing hit the bed he shimmied out of his boxers, turned and crawled to the middle giving Kale and Core a great view of his naked ass.

"Mmm, he does that on purpose."

Kale brought Core flush to his body by the waistband of his boxers. "He does and you love it. You and I are still overdressed." Hooking his thumbs in the band he pushed the fabric down Core's body letting it fall while sliding his hands back up to grip his hips. Kale's were discarded sometime during a heated kiss.

"You know what happens when you ignore me!"

Still pressed tightly together Core and Kale only turned their heads slightly to look at their bratty boyfriend.

"We have him so spoiled," Kale teased.

"Do it, Bing. Show us."

Bing spread his legs apart rubbing his hand up and down his chest before wrapping it around his erect cock. Tightening his grip he gave it one long stroke from root to tip. With closed eyes he repeated the action making himself moan from the pleasure.

"Fuck."

Bing smirked. They were so easy. 3, 2, 1…

The bed bounced from either side of him.

"Took you long enough."

His hand was knocked away from his needy cock as Cores took over. Hissing, Bing's hips shot up pushing his cock through Cores tight grip. Kale quieted his moans with a quick suck to his bottom lip before sliding his tongue in to caress his. Bing whimpered at the feel of Core licking his nipple and Kale grazing his teeth along his earlobe. Yes, together his men could silence the smartass.

"Please...more," Bing begged.

Core glanced at Kale and with unspoken agreement they decided. Core rolled him and Bing over so that Bing was on top. As their erections rubbed together deliciously both moaned hotly Core bringing Bing down for a heated kiss. Kale was soon behind Bing running his hands up and down his back and over the fleshy mounds of his perfect ass. Bing moved his hips to get some relief and spur Kale on.

Taking out the lube Kale poured some on his fingers. Rubbing one lubed digit over Bing's entrance he slowly pushed it in groaning at the tightness. As Kale worked on preparing him Bing added some lube to his and Cores erections giving them an easier slide as Bing slid his hips back and forth.

Kale reached down and brought Bing up so his back was flush to his chest. Tilting Bings head back Kale covered Bing's lips with his own as his hand ran down Bing's chest to find first his cock then Cores.

"You going to fuck Core while I fuck you, Bingy?" Kale asked licking his ear.

Bing's lust glazed eyes landed on Core.

Core licked his lips, "Up to you, baby. This is your show."

Bing's grin grew and he held out his hand, "Lube."

Bing's whole body tingled as his men made love to me. He may be the one in the middle, but Core still topped from the bottom and that was fucking A-OK. Bing was a spoiled brat. He knew it, they knew it, and they loved him anyway. No one would love them more than him.

He was going to come. Between Kale making it his mission to peg his prostate on every stroke Core was squeezing the hell out of his length.

"Keep doing what you're doing Kale our Bingy is close," Core panted.

"Me too."

Bing placed open mouth kisses all over Cores face, his lips eventually stopping on his. Core sucked on Bing's tongue as he felt that familiar twist in his belly.

"Fuck..." Bing screamed hoarsely as his orgasm slammed into him. He could feel Core still hard as a rock against his belly when Kale pushed him down further to chase his own relief.

Kale pulled Bing back up for a kiss as his body started to shake, and he flooded the condom.

"Core," Bing breathed against Kales lips. Kale was quick to pull out and so was Bing, both of them ditching the used condoms in the bedside trash.

Core waited patiently with his arm bent behind his head and his still erect cock leaking profusely on his belly.

Bing wrapped his tongue around the head licking up the tasty wetness before getting down to business. It wasn't time for teasing, their Core needed to come.

Core cursed as Bing swallowed most of his length in one go. Sucking cock is one of Bing's talents. Soon he had a hard, fast rhythm going, his only objective being draining his man dry.

"Please...don't stop...so close..."

At Cores' fingers tightening in Bing's hair he felt the first splash of warm liquid hit his tongue. Humming he milked Core until Core pushed his head away. Crawling up Bing was once again in the middle being cuddled.

“Thank you,” Core whispered with a kiss against my lips.

“Don't think you are off the hook, Core,” Bing warned although he’s grinning as he said it.

“Yes, Bingy.”

“Naptime,” Bing suggested.

“Yes.” Kale leaned over and kissed first Bing and then Core. “Love you both.”

Core does the same with Bing and Kale. “Love you both.”

“Love you both more.”

# NOT MY USUAL FLAVOR

“Schedule my usual for tomorrow night.”

Glancing down at the schedule she has open in front of her Reese gives her employer and friend a sly smile.

“You don’t want to try a new flavor this time?”

“Surprise me.”

As Journey St. James' personal assistant Reese is used to his odd behavior. She has been with him since he turned 21 and his acting career exploded. Journey is an out and proud gay man but he prefers renting his pleasure and makes this request about every two months. He told Reese one time over many delicious alcoholic beverages that trying to maintain a relationship in Hollywood was fucking exhausting. His ex had done a number on him with his constant jealousy and paranoia.

Journey started acting in his teens and now has over 100 television and film credits to his name. Not wanting to be typecast he has taken on a wide range of characters, straight or gay. His latest is that of fabulous Dirk Ryker private detective for hire. For the last three weeks he has been busy promoting the film and the next several months would be busy with a new project. He is looking forward to a night of relaxation and hopefully many orgasms that aren't acquired by his own hand.

"You got it boss. Now we need to hustle across town for that People interview."

"You lead the way and I'll follow you anywhere," Journey jokes, making Reese giggle.

He didn't know what he would do without his capable assistant. Hiring her had been the best decision he had ever made. Reese is damn good at her job and called him on his shit. Sometimes fame could go straight to your head and he needed to be called an asshole when he was being one. Best of all Reese was discreet and she didn't pry. She would patiently wait for him to spill his secrets to her. After seven years together Journey would have married the woman if he had been into women. He did consider her one of his closest friends.

***

Camden Theodore Elliott Bastions III or Cam was cursing his best friend in his head when he headed into Hotel Dumont's five star restaurant to meet a virtual stranger. Liam at the last minute called Cam and begged him to help him out. Supposedly Liam had a blind date lined up but couldn't make it due to work obligations. Liam couldn't reach the date and didn't want to stand him up. Cam only agreed because he needed a night out. His father had been hounding him again about taking over the family business, which happened to be ruling over a small unheard of country. Cam had no interest in the throne and wanted his father to hand it down to his sister. She would make a more appropriate King then he ever would. He was happy being a doctor and his country wasn't ready to have a gay King.

"Welcome to Splendor. Do you have a reservation?" the hostess asks as Cam steps up to the counter.

"It's under Liam Dunbar I believe."

"Yes, sir. The other person in your party has already arrived. He said to give you this." Cam blinks in confusion as the hostess presses a white envelope into his hand.

"Thank you." Stepping out of the way so the people behind him can move forward he finds a room key with a note inside.

Written in an elegant handwriting is a room number, 507. Somewhere in his head an alarm is sounding warning him to be cautious but curiosity gets the better of him as he decides to see what this is all about. As the elevator climbs to the fifth floor he has made every argument with himself about why this is a terrible decision. Meeting a stranger in a crowded restaurant is one thing, meeting a stranger all alone in a hotel room is stupid. Liam would never cause harm to him...he didn't think.

Cam nervously wipes his palms against his black slacks before lifting a shaking hand to tap at the door in front of him. Cam doesn't know what to expect as the door slowly opens revealing a tall, dark, and sexy man. Mr. Sexy is dressed casually in a pair of ripped jeans, a tight grey t-shirt, and a smile that should be illegal. His jet black hair is stylishly spiked up giving Cam a great view of chocolatey brown eyes. His dark complexion makes Cam wonder what nationality he is.

"You aren't what the agency usually sends but I did tell Reese to surprise me." The deep voice is like a seductive caress across Cam's body. "Please come in."

Cam is spellbound and the agency comment slips in one ear and out the other. Walking past the devastating man into the room Cam's nose is assaulted by a sweet spicy smell. Not only does he look good enough to eat, he smells utterly delicious. He still isn't sure what Liam has got him into but at the moment he has no complaints.

"My assistant usually sends me your file so I can see who you are, but today all I got was a name. It's Liam, right?"

"Um Cam...den actually, but everyone calls me Cam," Cam stutters softly. "Liam couldn't make it so I'm his replacement."

No one has ever affected him as quickly as the man before him.

"Nice to meet you Cam. Before we get started, would you like a drink?" He walks over to the mini bar and holds up a bottle of wine.

"Please." A drink would at least give him some time to figure out just what the hell is happening. "What is your name?"

Cocking his head to the side the hottie casts him an inquiring look. "The agency didn't tell you?" Sending a last minute replacement is rare for the agency but Journey trusted them completely. All the escorts had to sign confidentiality contracts at the time of hire. Some of the agency's clients were even more high profile than him. Since he likes what he has been sent he will let this oversight slide just once.

"Ugh, I was called at the last minute and told to meet you here. A name wasn't given," Cam explains feeling himself blush.

"You can call me Saint." Cam's breath quickens as Saint runs his finger down his cheek. "You are cute as fuck when you blush. I'm going to enjoy finding out just how far that pretty blush goes." Saint emphasized his words by trailing his finger down his chest and over the fly of his slacks.

Cam, in his head, knows he should be asking more questions but his heart says fuck it. It has been months since Cam felt a lover's embrace and his body wants the man before him like it needed oxygen. Rising up on his toes Cam captures Saint's lips with his own. Groaning at the taste of the sinful mouth Cam winds his arms around Saints neck deepening the kiss.

Saints body warms as their tongues duel in a sensual battle. Cam's flavor is intoxicating. When he opened the door he had been surprised to see what the agency had sent this time. His usual was the complete opposite of Cam. If he had to guess he would put Cam at around 5'6. Being over 6 feet himself he often asked for men around his same height and build. Saint had always been afraid of hurting someone smaller than him if he got too rough. Cam might be smaller but he could feel the strength in Cam's lean muscles as he gripped him.

He would admit to liking how Cam felt in his arms. Maybe his worries about hurting a smaller man had been in vain. Or maybe it just depended on the man. Pulling back from the kiss Saint stares into Cam's ocean blue eyes. His pupils are blown in passion and his breathing is labored. Picking him up Cam lets out the cutest squeak before locking his legs around his waist. Saint moans as their cocks rub together.

It feels fantastic even through the barriers of their clothes and he wants that barrier gone...like right now. Carrying Cam to the bed he drops him playfully earning him a giggle. Cam's shock of white hair falls into his eyes and Saint can't resist rubbing a few of the silky strands between his fingers before tucking the bangs behind an ear.

"You are beautiful," Saint whispers in awe.

"So are you."

Cam's hungry gaze follows Saint as he slips his t-shirt off and unbuttons his jeans revealing a perfectly sculpted chest. Smooth tan skin accompanied by abs Cam wants to trace with his tongue, so he does. Scooting to the edge of the bed Cam flicks his tongue out leaving wet trails as he tastes all that warm yummy skin for the first time.

Saint threads his fingers through Cam's hair to steady himself and guide him where he wants him. Which is lower, much lower. Smiling against Saints belly button he starts working on getting him naked. Running his open palm along the impressive bulge elicits a moan from the bigger guy.

Not able to wait any longer, Saint discards his boxers while pushing the weeping head of his dick onto Cam's pouting lips.

"Suck it…"

If he insists. Opening his mouth Cam takes him in halfway before retreating and repeating the action. Saints fingers tighten in his hair and Cam relaxes letting Saint use his mouth to seek his pleasure. Just watching his cock disappear and reappear between perfect plump lips is enough to bring him to the edge. Not wanting to spill too soon Saint steps back giving Cam a moment to take in a gulp of air.

"You...naked...now," Saint pants while dragging Cam's shirt over his head. Before Cam is able to untangle his limbs from the offending fabric Saint falls on him attacking his neck with open mouth kisses. The nip of teeth to his collar bone has him grinding his hips with abandon. His slacks need to go.

“Not naked...need...fuck,” Cam groans as a warm tongue licks his nipple.

“I’ve got you,” Saint murmurs as he works on opening Cams pants while giving the other nipple equal attention. Once Cam is naked Saint takes a moment to really look at him. Like he thought, long and lean. The tattoo of a phoenix on his chest is a surprise but this man seems to be full of them.

As Saint bends his head towards Cam’s hardness he is stopped by a tug on his hair.

“Blow jobs are great and all but can we skip ahead to the other fun stuff?”

“You are full of surprises,” Saint laughs against Cam’s parted lips.

Even to himself, Cam thinks. This man is bringing out the slut in him.

“Don’t move.”

“No worries,” Cam winks as Saint gets up and moves over to the dresser. Pulling a few items from the top drawer he is once again pressing Cam into the mattress. Cam can see that condoms and a bottle of lube have been set down by his head. Flipping the lid, Saint pours some of the liquid onto his fingers, settling one of his digits against Cam's entrance.

"You ready?"

Cam's answer is to press against the finger he wants sunk into his body.

"So eager...I like that."

"More," Cam begs as Saint moves his finger in and out adding a second. When he feels Cam is stretched enough he reaches for a condom that Cam snags from him.

"Let me do the honors," Cam says, ripping the little packet open with his teeth. Rolling it down Saints hard length Cam adds a healthy dose of lube. He hasn't done this in a long time and what he is about to receive is bigger than anything he's ever stuck up there. Cam is so ready for the challenge.

"You ready?" Saint asks once again.

Again Cam's answer is to cant his hips forcing himself onto Saints flared tip.

"I'm not going to ask again," Saint warns as he pushes forward, not stopping until fully seated in the tightest ass he has ever fucked. Saint was no saint so he had fucked quite a few asses since hitting puberty. Fame at times had its perks along with its downfalls.

"Move already or turn over so I can fuck myself!" Cam snaps. So much for giving him time to adjust.

"Bossy...I like that too." Rolling them over Saint barely has them settled as Cam slams his ass down drawing a moan from himself and a shout from Saint. Today had started off like every day for Cam. Woke up, went to work, tried a new place for lunch, but now he is going to die in ecstasy. At least he would die with a smile on his face.

"How the hell are you so tight?" Saint murmurs and Cam hopes he doesn't expect a coherent answer. All he is capable of right now is panting and an occasional moan. He is so close and when Saint grabs his hips to fuck him faster he reaches down to stroke himself to completion. When Saint feels the first hit of warm wetness on his belly it sends him over. Ignoring the mess Cam flops down on top of Saint boneless and sleepy. He should get up, wipe himself off, and find his clothes but he doesn't have the strength.

"That was...amazing," Saint whispers in awe like he can't believe it really happened. "I'm going to turn us so I can clean us up. You just rest."

Resting sounds perfect and Cam is all for it. Hearing a chuckle the bed moves as Saint rolls to his feet. A few minutes later he can feel a warm washcloth on his skin and a press of lips to his forehead.

Normally Saint is ushering his usual's out the door but tonight he wants to sleep next to this intriguing man. He has had great sex before but this was mind blowing. He isn't sure once will be enough which frankly worries him. He has never wanted seconds, ever.

***

Cam wakes as a ray of light hits his eyelids. Blinking them open he wonders for a second where the hell he is. Stretching his body he aches in places he hasn't in a very long time and he remembers what had transpired the night before. Sitting up to take a look around he finds he is alone. Part of him is relieved and part is disappointed. Cam has never had a one night stand. He knows in his heart that he won't see Saint again but last night will forever be burned in his memory. Knocking into the bedside table as he gets out of bed Cam notices the white envelope. Picking it up, inside he finds five hundred dollars and another note with elegant handwriting.

*Cam,*

*Thank you for introducing me to a new flavor. The pleasure was mine.*

*Saint*

Fuck…he needs to call Liam.

"Yo Cam!"

"We need to talk dumb ass. Now!"

"Sure I'll meet you at your house in twenty minutes."

Exactly twenty minutes later Cam and Liam arrive at his house at the same time. Cam met Liam almost six years ago when he first moved to the states to start medical school. At twenty three Cam wanted nothing more than to get out from under his father's thumb. His father hadn't wanted him to leave their country but his sister worked her magic talking their father into letting him with a promise that he would return before his thirtieth birthday. His time is running out.

Cam turns thirty in nine days and he knew his father had people watching him. Cam promised himself that he would never return. He had nothing against his country but he was free to be himself in the US. Here he is Camden Bastings and not Camden Theodore Eliott Bastions III. Growing up everyone treated him like he was made of glass. The Prince has a cold, put him to bed. The Prince scratched his arm, call the royal doctor. The Prince was found making out with a boy, marry him off to a Princess. He likes being Camden Bastings, regular guy or Doctor to his patients. He has no plans on going back to being a fragile Prince.

"Liam! Talk, now!"

"Sure but first how was the sex with Hollywood superstar Journey St. James? Which you can never talk about to anyone else by the way. I signed a gag order."

"I had sex with Journey St. James?" Cam knew he had looked familiar, but never in a million years would he have guessed Saint was Journey St. James.

"I knew he would be incredible. He was my birthday present to you besides your ass needed a good fucking," Liam says with a laugh.

Cam stands abruptly causing his chair to tumble backwards. "My birthday present? Are you insane? You sent me in your place to have sex with a virtual stranger." Throwing the envelope at Liam the money falls out onto the floor. "What is the going rate on a rent boy these days? Must be pretty high considering how much he tipped."

"Fuck, he must have liked you. He has never tipped that much, ever."

"Out of everything I said that is what you are focusing on! When did you start whoring yourself out, Liam? Don't you worry about your safety or mine? He could have been a rapist killer."

"Relax all the clients of the agency are well vetted. I feel safer with one of them than any random hook up. The pay is fantastic," Liam says while rubbing his hands together.

"When did you start this? We have been friends for years. I think I would remember you telling me about this career path," Cam yells in exasperation.

"About three months ago. I promise that it's all legit. I even get pay stubs and a W-2."

"How? Prostitution is illegal."

"The Agency is an escort service that specializes in companionship, giving their clients the boyfriend experience. Clients aren't paying for sex but the time being spent on them. If the client and the escort have sexual relations that is because they both agree on it, not because it is a paid service," Liam explains with a shrug.

"What a bunch of bullshit. Saint expected sex not my witty personality."

"Do most of our clients use our service for sex? Sure, but a good majority are lonely people wanting companionship. It is an escort's choice when it comes to accepting a job that will most likely end in sex. Cam I've made almost $20,000 in just three months. I've only had sex with three of the clients I was assigned to. The rest just want my company. I'm sorry for not telling you and tricking you yesterday but at least tell me it was worth it."

Cam considers lying but the smile that breaks free ruins that plan. "Yesterday was fucking amazing. The sex was the best I have ever had. I'm still mad at you for what you did though."

"I can live with that. Happy Early Birthday, Cam."

It was a happy early birthday, indeed.

***

"Reese, clear my schedule this weekend and I want the same flavor I had last time."

Reese stares at Journey in shock. It has only been seven days and he never asks for the same flavor. Ever. "He must have been something else," Reese observes. The small smile on Journey's lips confirms that.

"Tell the agency to send him to my cabin and I will be out of reach for the full 48 hours."

"Sure, boss. I'll make sure that the cabin is cleaned and stocked with food and other supplies," Reese says with a wink.

"That is why you are the best and I love you."

"I'll be sure to give myself a raise."

"You do that," Journey says with a laugh.

Liam can't believe his ears when he gets the call from the agency letting him know his service has been requested for the second time by Mr. Journey St. James.

"You must have really done a number on him," Mel the agencies owner says. "He has never requested a repeat. Make sure to give him the royal treatment this weekend. He's paying top dollar."

What Mel didn't know was that he had been given the royal treatment already. It isn't every day you get to have sex with a Prince.
"Hey Cam, what are you up to this weekend?" Liam asks over the phone.

“I'm working...like usual. Why?” Cam asks cautiously.

“You need to call off. Your Hollywood stud has requested your presence at his cabin for the entire weekend! Do you know how much money I'll be making?!” Liam shouts excitedly.

A whole weekend with the sexy actor? His body tingled just thinking about it.

“Fine, but this is the last time. You're going to get caught and I have a feeling lying to a client of your agency won't be looked upon too kindly.”

“Last time. I promise. I'll text you the address. You need to arrive by 10am on Saturday. He will be expecting you.”

After work on Friday Cam spends his evening packing a bag for the weekend and arguing with himself about how once again this is a terrible idea. The truth is Cam wants to see Saint again. He hasn't went a day without thinking about him or waking up in messy sheets from having dreamt about him.

Cam leaves his house on Saturday morning before 8am. He has about a hour drive and wants to give himself plenty of time just in case he gets lost. Pulling into a driveway he believes will lead him to the cabin he isn't prepared for what he finds. When Cams thinks cabin he pictures a small rustic type dwelling. This place has the look with its log exterior but it's bigger than most people's houses.

Guess he should have expected that when the owner is a superstar.

Taking a deep breath to calm his nerves Cam shuts his car off and gets out. Not bothering with his luggage he heads to the door and presses the doorbell. A few minutes later the door opens revealing once again a casually dressed Saint in jeans and a t-shirt. Cam would have preferred him naked, but I guess you can never be too careful these days. He wondered if he got hounded by paparazzi. He had his fair share of pics in the tabloids but most of them were from different functions.

Not able to contain himself Cam jumps into Saints arms crashing their lips together in a brutal kiss. Groaning Saint captures Cam's round bottom in his hands picking him up to carry him inside. Closing the door with his foot Saint presses Cam against the smooth surface of the door.

"What have you done to me? I can't stop thinking about you," Saint growls between mind numbing kisses.

"I can say the same thing," Cam accuses. "You have been staring in my dreams."

Saint's smile at hearing those words is blinding. "Don't worry you are the leading man in my dreams too."

Working quickly they tear each other's clothes off while impressively keeping their mouths fused together. Since Saint is wearing a tee and not a button up like Cam they finally break apart to get it over his head. Dropping to his knees, Saint doesn't ask for permission as he swallows Cam down in one go. Throwing his head back Cam almost knocks himself out having forgotten he is plastered against a hard surface. His hands find Saints shoulders for something to hold onto. Maybe he shouldn't have stopped him last time from blowing him. His mouth is perfect drawing his orgasm to the surface.

"You better stop!" Instead of heading his words Saint ups the ante by shoving a finger up his ass. Cam would have protested if it hadn't felt so damn good. Saint had the decency of coating his digit in salvia first. The burn is minimal and when he hits his sweet spot Cam sees stars. Saint is trying to kill him and the weekend has just begun. Not stopping he adds a second finger and then a third. The gentle suction on his spent cock is making it plump up again. He is pretty proud of himself. Normally he needs time between orgasms but today all he wants is more. Soon he is being spun around, his hands finding purchase against the wooden door. One minute he is missing Saints warmth and in the next a hard insistent thickness is driving into him making him scream.

Saint is beyond asking Cam for permission and he's sure Cam wouldn't appreciate it if he did. He pounds into him at a fast pace.

"How can you feel so incredible?" Saint wonders slipping an arm around Cam's waist to keep him from falling into the door.

Cam doesn't understand how Saint can form complete sentences. Cam is overwhelmed by the pleasure and all thoughts have left his brain other than, MORE. His hand is a blur as he strokes his cock. The orgasm that slams through him is even more intense than the last. Before his knees give out all he can think is he should apologize for the mess on Saints door. Catching his boneless lover Saint holds him up against his chest as his orgasm washes over him. Kissing his neck, Saint presses his sweaty forehead between Cam's shoulder blades. He has a feeling that this man will be the death of him.

"We need a shower and some food. I'm starving. Can you walk?"

When Cam wobbles he is swept up into strong arms. "I've got you, plus I know the way."

"Onward my prince," Cam teases.

More stolen kisses and playful caresses are exchanged in the shower than actual scrubbing but by the time the water runs cold they are both clean enough.

Peering into his fridge Saint is pleased to see that Reese has it stocked with all his favorites. He isn't much of a cook but he can make a killer omelet. Grabbing the eggs and other ingredients needed he turns to Cam and asks, "Are omelets okay?"

"That sounds great. Would you like some help?"

The next hour they work together companionably chopping up veggies, whisking the eggs, and finding the bread for toast. The conversation flows easily as they eat at the kitchen island. The more he learns about Saint the more he likes him. Do not fall in love with this man, Camden! All you are to him is a paid lay.

"Are you feeling okay?" Saint asks in concern at seeing Cam's pained expression.

"Yeah, I was just thinking I was an idiot for not recognizing you. I'm sorry I must have seemed daft."

"Honestly it was nice that you didn't seem to know me. I could just be Saint with you and not Journey St. James."

"I know the feeling," Cam murmurs. Tomorrow he would turn thirty and he knew his father would be coming for him. He is going to fight like hell to not go back to being Prince Camden.

"I've been meaning to ask you about your tattoo. Whoever did it does beautiful work."

"I got this after running away from home. It was a reminder of new beginnings," Cam explains.

"I'm sorry, Cam."

"Don't be. I've created a life I love here."

"So have I. I was born and raised in rural Illinois. My mom moved us to LA after my father passed away and I was scouted by a talent agent to be in a commercial. I get my pretty complexion from my mom's side. She is Polynesian. Every winter I wished we lived on the islands. I have been a few times to visit family but I've made LA my home."

"I miss my sister but that's about it. My home isn't the most tolerant towards people who are different."

"Sadly, most aren't. Progress has been made over the years but there will always be those who oppose it."

"True but I admire you for being out and not hiding who you are," Cam says sincerely.

"Even I hide sometimes, Cam. You have to have wondered why I choose to pay for company instead of dating. It's easier this way. The one man I ever loved couldn't deal with my career. He drove himself crazy and me along with him with his constant paranoia that I would leave him for one of my co-stars," Saint says sadly.

Cam squeezes Saints hand wanting to comfort him. "I think in any relationship you have to feel secure in your feelings. If you truly love that person you will put your trust in them. Until they do something to shake that trust you need to believe that you are the only one in their heart."

"Do you like to fish?"

Cam smiles at Saints topic for changing the current subject. “I do actually but I haven’t been in a long time.”

“Well it’s like riding a bike. Come on, I have a fully stocked pond. We can eat what we catch,” Saint blushes adorably. “As long as you know how to clean them that is.”

“I do know how. Let’s go.”

They spend the rest of the weekend fishing, hiking, skinny dipping, eating amazing food and having even more amazing sex. Cam wishes time would stop so he can stay tucked away with Saint longer.

“Thank you for this weekend. I will never forget it,” Cam says, giving Saint a hug before they part.

“I have a feeling we will be seeing each other again soon,” Saint murmurs.

Not likely, Cam thinks sadly. He isn’t going to be greedy and hope for more. He is already half in love with his sexy superstar. He also knows that if the truth were to get out that he isn’t an escort of the agency not only will Liam get fired but he doubts Saint would want him anymore.

“Take care of yourself okay.” With one last kiss Cam gets into his car and drives away. When he arrives home he finds his father and sister waiting for him. Several of his father’s guards are busy packing up his home.

“I’ve allowed you to be defiant for too long.  You will be coming home with us tonight.  I’m not taking no for an answer.”

Cam knows his father will make good on this threat.  He will go but it doesn’t mean that he will stay.  Cam realizes they need to work this shit out so he can resume his life here.

“I’ve missed you!  Happy Birthday!” his sister exclaims while pulling him into a hug.

“Me too.”  His sister is the oldest but by their laws the throne can only be handed down to the eldest son.  It is one rule Cam wants changed along with many others.  His country is on the cutting edge of many things but equality and sexuality are very much set in the past.

Cam manages to text Liam before his father has his phone taken away and he is whisked away to the airport.

***

“Journey St. James has once again requested your services.”

Shit!  It has been two weeks since Liam received Cam’s text that his father was basically kidnapping him.  With Cam several thousand miles away it’s not like he can fill in for him instead.  The charade is up and Liam hopes like hell he is still alive once he drops the bomb on one Journey St. James.

Journey stares at the handsome man across from him in confusion and anger. He didn't want to believe what he was saying.

"So let me get this straight. You work for the agency but decided to send your friend Cam in your place. As a birthday present?"

"Correct."

"The man that I can't stop thinking about is actually a prince. And a doctor. Did I mention a fucking liar?!" Journey growls.

"No, Cam actually never lied to you, he just didn't tell you the whole truth," Liam reasons.

"A lie is a lie is a lie. He lied by omission. He should have reported your ass after finding out what you did. I take my privacy very seriously and you sent me a stranger!"

"I'm a stranger."

Journey is ready to throttle this man. "A stranger that has had more background checks than common criminals. The Agency never hires someone without knowing everything about the person."

"I admit what I did was impulsive and wrong but I can see it in your eyes. You like Cam. I know that he likes you. Don't let what I did stop you from going after him."

Journey does like Cam. He probably would never have met him otherwise.

"I do like Cam. You are going to tell me where I can find him. When you leave here you will put your notice in at the agency instead of me turning you in," Journey commands.

"I will! Please bring my friend back."

***

"Father, please listen to us. Clarissa will be a much better ruler than me or even you for that matter. She wants to pull our country into the twenty-first century. Women need to be treated like equals. Men like me need to be free to love who they love. Please, father!"

It has been a month since his father brought him back and his father hasn't budged one bit.

"Just listen to what Clarissa wants to do for our country. Give her a chance before striking her down. I want to go home, father."

"You are home!" his father roars. "Renaldi is your home. Your people need you."

"No, father. Renaldi stopped being my home when I was told loving a man was immoral and forbidden. That I'm an abomination for how I feel. I'm not, father. The US has its flaws but they are way more accepting than Renaldi will ever be. I felt at home for the first time when I stepped foot on their soil. I'm free to be myself. I can't stay here!"

Henry's heart broke for his son. All he had ever wanted was for his children to be happy and his son to one day rule the country he loved. He knew that their ways are outdated, but it is hard to break centuries of habit. He knew how he could start.

"Clarissa, please show me what you would like to do."

"Really! Oh father, I want to do so much." Clarissa's excited smile warms his heart. As she animatedly starts her presentation their butler announces that they have guests.

"Liam! Saint! How are you here? Why are you here? Fuck it I've missed you!" Cam shouts, crushing the other man in a hug.

"I found out about you from Liam. I'm here for you. I can't seem to function without you."

"I'm here because I work for Saint now. I'm the personal assistant to the personal assistant. He took pity on me," Liam says with a smile.

"I mean how did you get into the palace?" The palace is heavily guarded.

"I invited him," his sister says, surprising him.

"Reese worked her magic and found out I'm pretty popular in your country. We reached out and I'm holding a couple fan events while I'm here."

"Camden, who is this young man?"

"My name is Journey St. James but my family calls me Saint. I have fallen in love with your son sir. I'm hoping you will allow him to come home," Saint pleads.

"I'm the best friend, Liam."

"All I have ever wanted was for my children to be happy. I didn't want to admit that my stubbornness was the cause of both their unhappiness. I want you to do what makes you happy, son. If that is resuming your life in the states then I give you my blessing. Please don't be a stranger. I would very much like to get to know your young man better."

Cam can hardly believe his ears. "Thank you, father. Clarissa is going to be an exceptional Queen."

"I do believe you are right. I hope you both stay for her coronation ceremony. I think it's time for us to shake our country up."

"Hi," Clarissa says shyly to her brother's best friend. "I look forward to getting to know you better."

Liam is too.

***

"Reese, schedule my usual for tonight at 7."

"Yes, boss."

"Give yourself another raise."

"On it boss."

At exactly seven there is a knock on the door. Saint smiles as he opens it, drinking in the sight of his husband. After eight years and two kids they still find time to recreate their first night together on their anniversary.

"Hey baby. Were the kids happy to see their grandfather and aunt Clary?" Saint asks after kissing his husband senseless.

"Ecstatic. They were playing with their cousins when I snuck out the door. We aren't expected back until tomorrow afternoon."

"Have I told you today that I love you?" Saint asks, walking them towards the bed.

"Yes, but I don't mind hearing it again."

"I love you. Thank you for showing up instead of Liam. I didn't know I had always been looking for you until I met you. Without you and our kids I am nothing."

"I would thank Liam again but I think him falling in love with my sister makes us even," Cam says with a wink.

"I agree...now let's forget our family for the next twenty four hours and focus on us."

"With pleasure."

## ABOUT THE AUTHOR

Lacey Ray is a native of Indiana, where she grew up enjoying all four seasons in one day. Her love of books lead to her career as a librarian. Her dream of becoming an author came true with her first published work, Aftermath. Happy Reading!

www.ingramcontent.com/pod-product-compliance
Lightning Source LLC
La Vergne TN
LVHW041039150826
845672LV00001B/382

* 9 7 9 8 8 3 9 6 7 5 3 8 4 *